# THE ICE HOUSE CAFE

# THE ICE HOUSE CAFE

CHINLE MILLER

Yellow Cat
PUBLISHING

ISBN: 978-0-9849356-8-0

Cover by Cary Cox

*For Aleksandra*

# CONTENTS

# 1

Bud Shumway settled down into the big purple-flowered cushions of the antique wicker chair, listening to the serene rippling of the nearby Crystal River. His dogs, Hoppie and Pierre, lay at his feet, also seeming to enjoy the peaceful sound.

Bud leaned back, relaxed and almost ready to nod off. Living in the little desert town of Green River, Utah, he wasn't used to the sound of running water, other than the slow occasional gurgle of an irrigation ditch on Krider's Melon Farm, where he was the manager.

About the only running water in Green River was the big slow-moving Green River, and it lacked the soothing chatter and murmur of the smaller and happier Crystal River here in the tiny village of Redstone, Colorado.

Bud loved his job as farm manager and had few regrets about quitting his job as Sheriff of Emery County some time ago due to burnout. And now that the fall watermelon harvest was over, he was enjoying being on vacation here in Redstone, where he and his wife, Wilma Jean, had rented a small cottage.

He pulled the chair forward to get a better view of the sparkling river that ran just below the cottage's full-length screened veranda lined with wicker furniture. The river really did seem to be made of crystal, the way the sunlight caught the tips of the whitewater. Watching the river was therapeutic, and it was nice to just kick back and take a break, especially after the hectic harvest.

But Bud did wonder what he was going to do to keep busy while they were here vacationing, though he had no doubts that Wilma Jean would conjure up something. His fears were more along the lines that such conjuring might involve shopping, especially since they weren't all that far from the glitzy town of Aspen.

Bud was suddenly wishing Howie, who had replaced him as sheriff, was here, along with his wife Maureen. Wilma Jean always took Maureen along on her junkets, leaving Howie and Bud to their own devices, of which they had plenty. It would be fun to take Howie's new metal detector up to some of the old mine dumps in the nearby mountains, Bud mused.

But Bud was on his own this time, as Howie was busy being sheriff, holding down the fort in Green River, a fort that Bud had sometimes thought resembled an outdoors insane asylum.

Now Bud accidentally scooted the chair into the dogs, waking them. They both quickly jumped up to avoid the chair legs, then decided they wanted onto Bud's lap, where things would be safer.

Hoppie, a Basset hound, tried to jump up, but his large body and short legs gave him an unmanageable center of gravity, and the little dog almost tumbled over.

Bud now leaned over and pulled him up while Pierre, a dachshund, jumped up and down on his short hind legs, managing to clear a few inches with each try, the proportion of clearance a bit askew for the length of his body. Bud next pulled Pierre up, and the little long dog sighed and squeezed down between Bud and the arm of the big chair.

This was just like in his big easy chair back in their Green River bungalow, Bud mused, thinking that some things never changed, no matter where one went. In this case, he was happy about that, as the dogs were like kids to him and his wife, though maybe like kids with rather simple minds and tastes. But he himself was a bit like that, Bud thought, rearranging Hoppie's hind legs so they didn't cut off his circulation.

It was October, and, just as he'd promised Wilma Jean, they had rented the little riverside cottage in Redstone, coming as soon as the melon harvest was done. They would stay for a month of relaxation in the tiny town known as the "Ruby of the Rockies" for its setting in the narrow valley under towering ruby-red cliffs. The town's main street, the Redstone Boulevard, ran the length of the town, following the contours of the river. It was lined with historic houses, many of which had been turned into tourist shops.

"What do you think of all this, boys?" Bud asked the dogs, making a sweeping motion with his arm that encompassed the big grassy lawn stretching to the riverbank, which was lined with narrow-leafed cottonwoods and box elders that glowed yellow in the evening sunset. "Sure is different from home, eh?"

Bud thought back to this, their third day in Redstone. He and Wilma Jean had enjoyed lunch at the Ice House Cafe, a small two-story house next door. It had once been a storehouse for large chunks of ice cut from the frozen river, providing refrigeration for the towns-people in the summer.

Bud had remarked to his wife how nice it would be to just walk next door for an espresso and blueberry scone each morning. He liked the little cafe, even though it had more of a touristy feel than Wilma Jean's cafe back home, the Melon Rind, and was much more upscale than the Chow Down, where he'd always gone for coffee and doughnuts when he'd been sheriff.

They'd enjoyed sitting in the cafe and watching the tourists walk by, but Bud had thought it kind of odd that the two women at the table near the front door had kept staring at Wilma Jean, though his wife hadn't seemed to notice. And what was even stranger was the note that one of the pair had surreptitiously slipped to Wilma Jean while on her way to the bathroom:

*It would be so nice if you'd give my mom a nod—she's one of your biggest fans. The table by the front door. Thank you!*

Wilma Jean, even though she had no idea what was going on,

turned and smiled and waved at the older woman, who then looked very self-conscious yet pleased, and managed to wave back as the younger woman smiled knowingly.

Wilma Jean had looked perplexed, but just shrugged her shoulders, whispering to Bud that it must be someone who had eaten in the Melon Rind back in Green River.

Still, it all seemed odd to Bud, as he'd never heard of anyone being a "cafe celebrity," and the pair had certainly acted like Wilma Jean was someone well-known.

But Bud hadn't dwelt on it, and by the time he and the dogs were kicked back in the big wicker chair in the cottage's veranda, it was all but forgotten.

# 2

After the incident at lunch, Bud and Wilma Jean had decided to walk the Redstone Boulevard, which they figured must be a popular tourist activity, from the looks of all the people.

They'd put the dogs on leashes, then stopped at the ice-cream shop to get ice-cream cones. Wilma Jean had to try the homemade honey jalapeño while Bud got his usual, vanilla bean, and the dogs each got a homemade doggie ice-cream biscuit. They then walked all the way to the end of the boulevard where the fire station sat on the banks of the river, let the dogs play a little in the grass, then headed back.

As they walked up the other side of the boulevard, Bud and Hoppie were trailing a bit behind Wilma Jean, who was leading Pierre, and Bud began to notice that she was getting more than her share of looks.

He knew his wife was attractive, but she didn't usually garner this much attention, and Bud wondered if there wasn't something about their dress or mannerisms that made people think they were different. After all, the little town of Green River definitely had its share of idiosyncrasies, and maybe they stood out and didn't realize it.

But Bud didn't think this was the case at all, as people seemed to be paying him no mind, so he decided it must be Pierre that was drawing all the attention. The little wiener dog actually was pretty cute with his pink rhinestone leash and matching collar.

But still, along with the note in the cafe, it had all seemed kind of odd.

As darkness fell, Bud still sat on the veranda, listening to the sound of the river and thinking about all this, and he soon began fiddling with the string of smooth beads in his pocket, beads that had arrived in the mail just a few days before he and Wilma Jean had left Green River.

Bud's great aunt, Minnie Mae, had passed away some months ago, and her daughter, Cindy Mae, had sent the necklace to Bud as a remembrance of his aunt, even though he hadn't been all that close to her.

Cindy had told him that the string of beads was the only thing that hadn't been claimed by the rest of the family for some reason, and would Bud like to have it? He'd said sure and didn't want to be ungrateful to her for thinking of him, but in reality, he wasn't sure what to do with the beads. Fortunately, he'd since found that the necklace made a great fiddling device, and he'd been in the market for such, having recently given up his pipe.

Bud was glad to be rid of the pipe, in all honesty, as he'd gotten tired of having everyone tell him he couldn't smoke, even though he never actually put anything in it. He'd used it to fiddle—all he wanted to do was think, something he just couldn't do very well without being able to fiddle with something.

And now, the beads were perfect in this regard, as nobody could tell what he was doing—he could just put his hand in his pocket and fiddle away, rolling the beads like a worry stone, nobody the wiser. Even Wilma Jean, who he drove crazy with his fiddling, hadn't noticed.

It was now almost pitch dark, and Bud suddenly felt Hoppie's little body stiffen, as if he'd seen something. Pierre was soon also awake and on full alert, and Bud strained to see through the shadows. At first, he thought it was probably just a rabbit coming out to graze on the grassy lawn, but the dogs saw rabbits frequently on their lawn back home and didn't act like this.

Bud could now see something over at the rear of the Ice House Cafe, something that looked like a person standing in the shadows. He wasn't able to make out much, but they appeared to be wearing a white dress or robe, the evening breeze blowing the material around them like gauze.

Now the shadowy figure stepped from behind the cafe where Bud could see it more clearly. It was definitely a woman, someone of slight build, and Bud was sure he could make out long dark hair against the billowy white garment.

Hoppie was now growling, and Pierre acted like he was ready to start barking, even though he was scrunched down too low along the chair's arm to be able to see anything and was, as usual, just going along with Hoppie. Bud put his hand around Pierre's mouth while telling Hoppie to shush.

The figure seemed to float above the grass and was soon standing on the bank of the river behind the cafe, looking like it might step into the whirling waters. He held his breath, wondering exactly who or what he was watching and whether or not they would step off the bank. If so, he knew they would immediately be swept away, as the river narrowed behind the cafe and was deep and swift there.

Bud stood just as the figure turned and appeared to float into the shadows of a clump of willows further up the bank, gone like a ghost in the night.

## 3

"Hon, you saw Lady Osgood's ghost last night," Wilma Jean informed her husband, raising a cup of coffee as if giving him a toast. "At least, that's what Hannah, the waitress, told me when I asked her about it while you were taking your time getting over here to the cafe."

"I was giving the dogs their Barkie Biscuits," Bud replied a bit testily. "You were going to run off and completely leave them on their own to suffer while we're over here eating opulent breakfasts."

Wilma Jean smiled, then added, "I'd already given them their biscuits, sweetie. They're con artists of the highest order, and you always fall for it. No wonder they're getting chubby."

Bud looked chagrined as Wilma Jean continued. "Anyway, Lady Osgood was the wife of John Cleveland Osgood, the industrialist who discovered coal around here in the 19th century and built the village of Redstone to house his miners."

Bud nodded distractedly. He liked history with the best of them but wasn't much impressed by ghosts, historical or not. Instead, he was wondering what his ex-deputy Sheriff Howie was up to. Even though he and Wilma Jean had been gone only a few days, he already kind of missed Howie's daily phone calls asking for advice, though he would never admit it, as he usually considered Howie's calls to be mostly unnecessary. More often than not, Howie just wanted to talk.

Hannah, the Ice House Cafe waitress, a petite and wiry woman who looked to be in her fifties, had come by and was refilling their coffee cups.

She'd obviously heard what Wilma Jean had said and added, "Lady Osgood was loved by everyone in the town. She was Osgood's second wife and was actually a for-real Swedish countess. Her name was Alma Regina Shelgrem. She was called 'Lady Bountiful' by the residents because she was always helping them out."

Bud toyed a bit with his cheese and asparagus omelet, thinking about Lady Bountiful. His pragmatic mind didn't much like the thought that he'd seen a ghost.

Hannah leaned over their table and said in a low voice, "People see her ghost, and then in the next day or two someone usually dies. Too bad you saw it."

Bud replied, "How often do people see it?"

"Oh, maybe once a month or so. She's usually seen more up around the Redstone Castle, which was where they lived, though they called it Cleveholm Manor, but sometimes people see her at the Redstone Inn. She's started being seen around town more recently, but this is the first time anyone's seen her near the cafe here. Kind of gives me the creeps, even in broad daylight. You mark my words, somebody's going to die. I just hope it isn't me."

"How many people live in Redstone?" Bud asked.

"Oh, I don't know, maybe around 100 or so."

"Well," Bud replied, "It's a wonder there are that many left, if this ghost is seen so often and then somebody dies."

Wilma Jean kicked him lightly under the table. "Hon, don't be such a skeptic. I'm sure Hannah here knows exactly what she's talking about."

Hannah nodded her head in agreement and replied, "I've lived here for five years, and this thing has been sighted as long as I've been here, I know that."

Bud asked, "Isn't it just residents who are affected by this? I mean, why would a complete stranger, like me, be subject to a local superstition, especially one visitors probably don't even know about?"

"Look," Hannah replied, putting the coffee pot on the table and sitting down in the booth by Wilma Jean, "I didn't believe a word of it when I moved here from Carbondale. I even laughed about it and said it was just a dumb legend. I didn't believe in ghosts for one minute."

She ran her hands through her long dark hair, then continued, "Truth was, my neighbor saw the ghost one night, and the next day, my cat nearly died. Just out of the blue, she ran out into the street and almost got hit by a car. I ended up giving her to my best friend before she got run over. Anybody and anything alive is subject to this thing. It's kind of like the old Ute curse."

"Ute curse?" asked Wilma Jean.

"The native Utes were forced out of this beautiful country, and they loved it so much they put a curse on it."

"How does that work?" asked Bud.

"Well," Hannah replied, reaching over and refilling his coffee cup without getting up. "They said that whoever came here was cursed to always want to come back. It's true. You just ask any of these gazillion tourists who come around. They always want to come back."

"No doubt," Wilma Jean replied. "It's a beautiful valley, and the town's very unique."

Hannah stood as a touristy-looking couple carrying cameras walked in the front door. She told them, "Sit anywhere you want," then turned back to Bud. "You go ahead and be skeptical. I don't blame you one bit. I was the same way. But you watch. Somebody's going to die."

She kind of shuddered, then handed menus to the bewildered tourist couple, who had obviously overheard what she said, then went back into the kitchen.

Suddenly, as if on cue, a siren blared its way up the boulevard, on past the Ice House Cafe, past the old historic Redstone Inn, and on down the road to the Redstone Castle. Bud couldn't see the vehicle from where he sat, and it was soon followed by another siren.

"That was an ambulance," said Wilma Jean soberly. "And a Pitkin County Sheriff vehicle. I could see their reflection in the side window. I hope nobody's died or anything like that."

Bud thought of how Hoppie and Pierre's scruffs had been up last night when they saw the supposed ghost.

He replied, "If someone died it wasn't because of a ghost. Dogs aren't superstitious, and they don't see ghosts. What we saw had to be a real person."

He then put his fork down, his appetite suddenly gone. For some reason, he had a hunch their vacation might turn out to be more interesting than he'd initially thought. His fears of getting bored were likely to vanish, just like a ghost.

# 4

In spite of the lure of the sirens, Bud had no interest in what was going on in the law enforcement arena in Redstone, or any other place for that matter, except maybe Green River, and he wasn't even too sure about that.

Even though he'd quit law enforcement to become a quiet peaceful melon farmer, murder and mayhem had seemed to follow him around, or at least sometimes it felt that way.

Some of that was because Sheriff Howie was always making sure Bud was on the inside track of whatever was going on. Bud didn't mind this for the most part, but this month here in Redstone was supposed to be his time off.

When October was over, he and Wilma Jean would go to his old stomping grounds of Radium, Utah where he would become a seasonal deputy, helping his friend Sheriff Hum Stocks. He would work there from November until it was time for the melon farming to start back up, probably sometime in March or April, depending on the weather.

As Krider's farm manager, Bud had really looked forward to having the winters off, something he hadn't been able to do as sheriff.

But last winter, which was supposed to be his first winter off, he'd instead ended up serving as interim sheriff in Radium County while his old friend Sheriff Hum Stocks was recuperating from an injury. After that, they'd returned to Green River, where he'd spent the remainder of winter helping Wilma Jean at her cafe and bowling alley, also spending some time on his hobby of photography. He'd eventually gotten bored, something he'd never expected.

But this winter would be different. Hum had badly wanted Bud to come down and help him out, and Wilma Jean had decided she wouldn't mind taking the winter off, as she was getting burned out with running her cafe and bowling alley, just like Bud had been with being sheriff. She and Bud had once both lived in Radium, and it would be nice to reunite with old friends.

Wilma Jean had hired Howie's wife, Maureen, who already worked for her part-time, to take over everything while they were gone. Maureen and Howie had moved from their tiny apartment into Bud and Wilma Jean's bungalow at the edge of town, saving the couple rent money and also taking care of the house so it wasn't sitting empty. It seemed like the proverbial win-win all around, Bud thought, and Wilma Jean had agreed.

But now that it was all set, Bud was kind of regretting signing on to work the winter for Hum, even though he remembered well enough the boredom he'd suffered. When he'd signed on, he'd been looking forward to getting back into law enforcement, but now that he'd just finished the harvest, he was tired and not looking forward to working for anybody.

His time here in Redstone was supposed to be spent doing nothing but exactly what he wanted to do, mostly puttering around and taking photos of the mountains, with a little exploration thrown in, though he wouldn't be going far off-road in Wilma Jean's pink Lincoln Continental.

He was regretting the decision to leave his old Toyota FJ at home. He'd studied some maps of the area the previous night after he'd seen the so-called ghost and hadn't been able to sleep. It looked like the rugged mountains had plenty of interesting four-wheel roads, and he wanted to check them out.

Maybe he could somehow take the train from the nearby town of Glenwood Springs back to Green River and get the FJ. It was a thought, and he knew he would enjoy the train ride, as he loved the big noisy behemoths and the clickety clack of their wheels.

The sirens had now faded away in the distance. It was time to get the dogs and drive to McClure Pass, where he and Wilma Jean had planned to have a picnic after a hike in the aspens.

It would be a good opportunity for Bud to get some photos of the beautiful West Elk Mountains in all their autumn glory, the aspens turning red and gold. Though quickly fading, some of the lower altitude scrub oak was still showing color, and Bud was eager to try a new polarizing filter he'd bought.

As they left the Ice House Cafe, Hannah the waitress followed them out. She looked excited.

"I've been in the back listening to the police scanner, and my friend Denise just called me. Word's out that Callie Jensen was found dead in the bushes outside her bedroom deck by the groundskeeper. Denise thinks she was murdered."

Hannah paused to take in the look on Bud and Wilma Jean's faces, then asked, "Say, where did you guys say you're from?"

Bud replied, "Utah—Green River, Utah. Why?"

Hannah looked at Wilma Jean. "When I first saw you, I thought you were Callie. You look just like her from a distance, but when you got up closer, I could see you weren't. Callie bought the Redstone Castle several years ago, and just like Lady Osgood, everyone around here liked her, she was so generous. I can't see why anyone would murder her."

Hannah paused, then added, "By the way, you might know her by her stage name—Calico Callie—you know, the famous country-western singer. But do you think whoever murdered her might have been after you and mistook her for you? Do you have any enemies who might have followed you over here? In any case, I hope we don't have her ghost wandering around town now along with Lady Bountiful's. I just knew someone was going to die."

Hannah opened the door of the Ice House Cafe, turned and gave Bud an "I told you so" look and went inside. Just then, an SUV bearing the emblem of the Pitkin County Sheriff drove up.

# 5

Two deputies got out of the sheriff's vehicle and nodded at Bud and Wilma Jean, then went into the cafe. The deputies were soon back in the SUV with cups of coffee and doughnuts, heading in the direction of the Redstone Castle.

It felt kind of strange to Bud to not know the officers, since he knew everyone in his little town of Green River, though it reminded him of a time when he'd wished he hadn't known any of the local lawmen.

Though Bud was in high school up the road in Price, Utah, he'd been visiting his grandparents in Radium, and one of his buddies there, Buster Dalton, had taken him for a joyride on his uncle's "borrowed" tractor. The pair had soon been stopped by the long-time Radium Sheriff, Buckshot Williams, Hum's predecessor.

Buster's uncle had decided not to press charges if Bud and Buster agreed to spend a few weeks helping him on his farm, which included the hard work of helping buck in the fall hay harvest—all without pay.

Bud had decided it was a heck of a price to pay for a joyride and refused to engage in any further shenanigans with Buster, of which there would be many. Buster finally changed his ways and became a law officer up in Price.

Bud figured Buster was probably one of the more empathetic peace officers on the force, primarily because Buster himself had been there, done that. He'd even spent a day in jail for wiring a speaker onto the front of his car that would blast out a siren when he wanted to run stop lights. In any case, he later went on to eventually be voted in as Sheriff of Carbon County, where he could turn on his siren and run lights with impunity.

Before that, Bud had typically had only good associations with the law business, as his other grandfather up in Price had been Sheriff of Carbon County while Bud was growing up, long before Buster held that same office.

Now, back at the cottage, Bud opened the door, and Pierre dove for his pant leg, grabbing on and dragging across the floor, while Hoppie excitedly wagged his tail and growled, egging Pierre on. Bud headed for the kitchen, where he extricated himself from the little dog's death grip by sidetracking him with a Barkie Biscuit.

"It's pure extortion," he said in his own defense as Wilma Jean gave him a look with raised eyebrows. "If he gets fat enough, he won't be able to hold on, and he'll naturally thin down again because I won't have to give him a biscuit, so not to worry."

Bud wondered what it must be like to be a dog and be dependent on people for everything, especially treats, and he decided he wouldn't like it very much.

On the other hand, he wouldn't have to worry about anything, just whether or not he would be getting many treats that day. And if he were smart, like Pierre, he could figure out a way to get exactly what he wanted, so maybe it wouldn't be such a bad life after all.

And it might actually be kind of fun hanging his head out the window of Wilma Jean's big pink Lincoln and barking at people as she drove down the street. He'd have to try it out sometime, he thought—someplace where nobody knew him.

Just then, Bud's phone rang, and he could tell from the caller ID that it was Sheriff Howie, back in Green River. Bud felt a sense of familiarity as he answered the phone—Howie was calling him again. All was right with the world, in spite of whatever had just happened at the Redstone Castle.

"Yell-ow," Bud answered.

"Sheriff, that you?" Howie asked. Though it usually mildly irritated Bud that Howie still called him sheriff, this time he didn't mind.

"Yup. What's up, Sheriff?" Bud replied.

"Well," came the reply, and then Howie paused, just as he always did, thinking of what he was going to say, not one to quickly jump into anything—or so Bud thought, giving Howie the benefit of the doubt.

Bud waited awhile, then finally asked, "And?"

Wilma Jean had collected the picnic items and was giving him a look that said she was ready to go.

"Well," Howie repeated. "I hate to bother you on vacation over there. Say, what's it like? I've never been to Colorado, and just yesterday me and Maureen were talking about how nice it would be to take a little vacation, assuming I could get away, which I probably can't, seeing hows there's nobody here to cover me."

"It's beautiful, Howie. Lots of nice cool mountains and a sparkly river running right through everything. It would be great if you could come over, but what would you do with Bodie and Tobie?"

"Oh, we talked about that. We could leave them for a short time, and Krider's daughters could check on them. The cats are loving it here at your bungalow, by the way."

"Glad to hear it, Howie. Everything OK?"

"Yeah, you should see Bodie. Man, is that cat crazy. You know, I got a laser penlight like the director of that Shakespeare play that was here had, and man, that cat chases that thing all over the house. It's a bright red light shaped like a star, kind of cool. Bodie even managed to jump up on the top of the fridge one time when I pointed it up there. Maureen saw him and read me the riot act about him being up on the counters, though, so don't mention it to Wilma Jean. He almost knocked your Scooby Doo cookie jar off."

"I won't say a word, Howie. But say, we're about to take off here on a picnic. What's up?"

"Well, Sheriff, I'm kind of embarrassed about this, but I need your help 'cause I don't know what to do."

"No need to be embarrassed, Howie."

"Oh, I'm not embarrassed about needing your help, that's nothing new. I'm embarrassed about *why* I need your help."

"Oh?" Bud asked, patiently waiting, though he was starting to wonder if Howie would ever get to the point.

Howie now began softly counting, "One-thousand one, one-thousand two..."

"Howie, why are you counting?"

"I dunno, Bud, that's just what you always do when you're waiting for me to spill the beans. I thought I'd save you the trouble and do it for you for once."

Bud grimaced. He hadn't been aware Howie had heard him counting while he waited.

"Anyway," Howie continued, "I guess I have to get it out sooner or later, so it might as well be sooner."

"Get what out?" Bud was now beginning to feel that old familiar feeling of frustration, but for some reason, it felt almost welcome. He must be a bit homesick to actually enjoy Howie's beating around the bush, he decided.

Finally, in a barely audible voice, Howie replied, "Well, Sheriff, you know how I always left a spare key in a Hide A Key thingy under the bumper of the Land Cruiser? I had no choice, 'cause I'm on my own here, with nobody to back me up, so if I ever lost my keys..." His voice trailed off.

"You lost your keys to the sheriff's vehicle?" Bud asked.

"Worse than that, Bud," Howie said grimly.

"How much worse, Howie?"

"Way worse. Somebody found the key and stole it."

"Stole the key?"

"Well, yeah, they stole the key, but the bad thing is that they just

happened to have it in the ignition of the Land Cruiser when they
stole it."

Bud groaned in disbelief.

"Anyway, Bud, I need to go. I have a bad headache. No idea why,
as I never get headaches."

"OK, Howie, take care of yourself," Bud responded, but he wasn't
sure if Howie had heard him, as Howie had already hung up.

# 6

"It appears that the Sheriff of Emery County had his vehicle stolen," Bud said as Wilma Jean looked at him questioningly.

"What?" she asked incredulously. "Howie had the Land Cruiser stolen? It's almost new. I hope somebody didn't take it joyriding and wreck it. Why would someone steal a sheriff's car?"

"I'm sure it's happened before," Bud replied. "Just never in Emery County. And Howie's hoping to be elected into office next month, so his constituents might now wonder if that's the right thing to do or not."

"I bet some of them aren't wondering at all," Wilma Jean answered.

"Well, I think he's done a pretty good job since I left him holding the bag. He had only a few months' experience. People need to remember that he was a cook before that."

"I'm sure they remember," Wilma Jean said wryly.

"I thought people mostly liked him," Bud said.

"They do," Wilma Jean replied. "At least those who come into the Melon Rind say they do, in general. But I think a few question his competence."

"He solved the murder of that guy up in Price."

"I think it's more along the lines that your shoes as ex-sheriff are a bit hard to fill."

"I do just fine," Bud said, looking down at his Herman Survivor boots, noting they still had a bit of irrigation mud on them.

Bud thought back to how Howie had recently walked the streets of the town, shaking hands with virtually every single one of his constituents, then telling Bud he was going to win even though he had no election war chest. He'd also gone to the other small towns in the county, such as Castle Dale, and shaken plenty of hands there. Of course, it helped that he was running unopposed, but nothing was guaranteed.

This in turn reminded Bud of his Uncle Junior, who had been upfront and just bribed everyone in his run for mayor of the little town of Paradox, Colorado, giving them all free Eskimo Pies when they came into his general store.

Wilma Jean asked, "What's Howie going to do now?"

Bud replied, "I was going to tell him to file a report with the sheriff's office, but I decided it wouldn't be very funny, since he *is* the sheriff's office and he's worried sick. He's put out an APB and is now going to have to drive that old Crown Vic we used before Krider donated the money for the Land Cruiser—Krider along with Doc Richardson. Say, you heard from Doc and Millie lately?"

"Funny you ask. I called them to tell them we would be coming through Palisade, but they were gone. But they called yesterday and want to come visit while we're here, since it's not too far."

"That would be great," Bud replied. "But Doc won't be happy to hear that the object of his donation was stolen. At least it's insured, or so I hope. Howie's not the greatest with paperwork."

"He sure has plenty of time to read those old *Lost Treasure* magazines and go up to the old missile range with his metal detector."

"You sound like you're mad at him."

"I am."

"Why?"

"He went home drunk last night."

Bud was shocked. "Howie? Our mild-mannered straight-laced Sheriff Howie?"

"The one and the same. He went home late, almost drove into the fence, then stumbled inside and acted like nothing was different, except he fell into bed with his clothes on."

"Who told you all that?"

"Maureen. She said he smelled like alcohol. She's mad at him, too."

Bud shook his head in disbelief. "I can't imagine what got into him. That's not at all like him."

"That's exactly what Maureen and I think. Do you suppose the stress of being sheriff is getting to him?"

"Well, he won't have any stress if he does *that* more than once, because he won't *be* sheriff," Bud replied.

They were soon in Wilma Jean's Lincoln, driving down the boulevard, Wilma Jean driving, Hoppie in the middle, and Pierre in Bud's lap on the passenger side.

As they came alongside a little kid riding his bike, Bud leaned out the window and barked, "Woof, woof, woof." The kid stopped in surprise, then smiled and waved as Hoppie and Pierre began barking at him out the window.

Wilma Jean laughed. "Bud Shumway, what's come over you?"

"I accidentally ate a Barkie Biscuit this morning," he replied. "Actually, I've always wanted to see how much fun that would be, since the dogs get to do it all the time."

"Was it fun?" she asked, now turning the big car onto the highway and toward McClure Pass, which was up the road a few miles.

"It was, but maybe a bit overrated."

Bud stroked Pierre's long nose, and the chubby little wiener dog stretched out and went to sleep, Hoppie soon following suit, his head in Wilma Jean's lap.

As they drove up the scenic Crystal River Valley, following the happy little river, Bud thought about Howie coming home drunk. It was worrisome and totally out of character, and Bud knew something unusual had to be going on.

They soon passed the extensive grounds of the Redstone Castle on the other side of the river, and Bud caught a glimpse of the big English Tudor manor house through the trees. It wasn't really a castle at all, but probably seemed like one to the hard-working and poor coal miners.

"Look, hon, the castle," Wilma Jean pointed, then added, "Hannah said the large stone blocks they used came from just across the river here, from these big red sandstone cliffs. Osgood used the finest craftsmen of his time to build and decorate it—even Tiffany and Stickley were involved. It has 24,000 square feet and 42 rooms. I wish we could tour it sometime, but it's that singer's private home."

"I hope she wasn't really murdered and instead had an accident or something," Bud replied.

"I can't imagine why people would kill each other," Wilma Jean replied. "Except when I think of Howie going home like he did last night, and then I understand."

"I'm wondering if I shouldn't ride the train back home, check up on Howie, and get my FJ," Bud said. "I wouldn't mind taking it up into the high country and doing some exploring.

As they came around a corner, he said, "Hey, pull over! The sign says there's a waterfall here—Hays Creek Falls."

Wilma Jean quickly steered the big car to the side of the road into a wide pullout above a little creek that dropped down a narrow gorge into the Crystal River.

They left the dogs in the car and followed a somewhat precarious pathway along the creek until they reached a small waterfall tumbling down the canyon wall, threading through the trees and bushes like an airy strand of silver light.

It seemed almost ethereal to Bud, especially compared to anything he'd seen in the desert, with the golden aspens and red chokecherry leaves making the perfect frame for the white bubbling water. He wondered what it was like in the spring—the snowmelt probably made it thunder over the edge and spray everything all around with ice water.

Bud thought about getting his camera, but figured the contrast between the light and shadow would make it difficult to photograph, and besides, he was happy just soaking it all in.

He turned to say something to Wilma Jean, but she had disappeared. Just like Howie's Land Cruiser over in Green River, his wife was mysteriously gone.

# 7

Bud figured Wilma Jean had gone back to the car for some reason, though it wasn't like her to not say something. He turned and headed back down the trail, when he saw a flash of red through the trees.

Someone was coming, and it wasn't Wilma Jean, as they were wearing red, and she'd been wearing blue jeans with her favorite t-shirt, the white one with the words, "Never Judge a Book by its Movie."

Even though Bud knew this was probably a popular spot for tourists, he felt an instinctive urge to hide in the trees. For some reason, his intuition was telling him something was off.

He slipped into the aspens lining the trail, then crouched down into the shrubby understory. Sure enough, someone was coming up the trail. It was a woman and a man, and they didn't seem to Bud like they were at all interested in the falls, but were looking for something.

They stopped right in front of where Bud was hiding, and he could now see that the woman was Hannah from the Ice House Cafe. She was with a scruffy looking man who appeared to be in his 50's, just like Hannah. He was short and a bit chubby with a scruffy beard and wore a white t-shirt with baggy jeans that looked like they might fall off any second.

Hannah said, perplexed, "Where'd they go? They left their dogs in their car, so they couldn't be planning to go far."

"Dunno," answered the man. He pointed ahead on the trail, "They probably climbed up to the top of the falls. Are you OK, Hannah?"

"How can I return what's hers if we can't find her?" Hannah asked with concern.

Bud's senses said to stay still. He had no idea what Hannah was talking about. He had no idea why they were looking for Wilma Jean, but he felt no need to reveal himself until he knew more.

He instinctively felt for his shoulder holster with its Ruger, but he hadn't even thought of bringing it on a picnic. Instead, he now went for the string of beads in his pocket, silently spinning them on their silver string.

The pair continued on up the trail, and now Bud felt a strong sense that something was definitely off. Where was Wilma Jean? The pair hadn't mentioned seeing her, so she couldn't have gone back to the car.

He stepped back out and looked off the edge of the ravine gouged into the terrain by the creek, thinking maybe Wilma Jean had slipped and was on the bank below the trail. He scanned up and down the rocky rubble, but saw nothing.

Now he was beginning to get really worried. He started back down the trail toward the car. She had to be somewhere between here and there—if she'd passed him, he would've seen her. The car wasn't far, and on the way back down, he stopped to occasionally look over the bank.

He was almost back when he thought he heard something and stopped. The creek below was very roily as its small rapids crashed over the rocks, making it hard to be sure.

He thought that maybe it was Hannah and her friend coming back down the trail, so he again stepped off to the side.

As Bud pushed the foliage aside, he looked up, and he couldn't believe his eyes—there was Wilma Jean, leaning against a big aspen tree, rubbing her ankle, looking like she was in pain.

Bud was soon by her side, helping her.

"What happened?" he asked.

"I saw a bunch of blue columbine up here in the trees. You'd already gone ahead, so I decided to climb up and look at them, then catch up with you. I slipped on the wet grasses coming back down and sprained my ankle. It really hurts."

Bud could see her ankle was red and already starting to swell. He carefully helped her down the slope to the trail, then they headed back to the car.

He felt a sense of urgency and soon had Wilma Jean in the passenger side and was turning the big car around and heading back to Redstone. A red Toyota hatchback Celica that appeared to be from the 1980s was parked nearby.

"What's the hurry?" Wilma Jean asked.

"Did you see Hannah and her friend on the trail?"

"No. They were there?"

"Yes, and they were looking for us."

"Did you talk to them?"

"No, I hid."

"Hid?"

"I felt uncomfortable, like they were up to something."

"Bud, Hannah's a very nice person. Why would she be up to something? And what could she possibly be up to? We barely even know her. And if you didn't talk to her, how do you know she was looking for us?"

"I heard them talking. She said something about returning something that was yours. I think she had you confused with someone else. I just felt something was off."

They were soon back to town, and Bud pulled up in front of the cottage and took the dogs inside, then came back and helped Wilma Jean in.

As he shut the front door, Bud noticed the same red Celica that he'd seen at the waterfall pull up in front of the Ice House Cafe, let Hannah out, then drive away.

He watched as Hannah unlocked the cafe door and turned the "Closed" sign to read "Open," then stood for a long time on the front steps, looking toward Bud and Wilma Jean's cottage, before finally going inside.

# 8

"Is that Calico Callie?" Bud asked Wilma Jean, who was stretched out across the couch watching TV, her ankle wrapped in a bandage with an ice pack over it.

Neither Bud nor Wilma Jean were big television fans, though Bud always enjoyed watching his favorite show, Scooby Doo, and Wilma Jean liked to watch the Cooking Channel once in awhile, as well as old Sherlock Holmes mysteries.

Wilma Jean hadn't done much since yesterday when they'd been at Hays Creek Falls, and Bud had just gotten them some fried chicken and macaroni salad for lunch from the little market down the street. Neither had been back into the Ice House Cafe.

"Yes, that's Calico Callie," Wilma Jean replied. "The Aspen station is doing a tribute to her in memoriam. She lived there before buying the castle and had lots of friends. They just had an interview with the Pitkin County Sheriff, and he says she was definitely the victim of foul play, though he didn't say how she died."

"That's standard when they're doing an investigation," Bud replied. "They can't say much. Boy, she looks enough like you to be your twin sister."

"She does, doesn't she? Kind of eerie. And I can't believe someone would kill her. And right when we get to Redstone. Then I have to go wreck my ankle so I can't do anything. I'm about ready to go home, hon."

"We can't go home. Our home is occupied by the Emery County Sheriff and his wife. Have you talked to Maureen today? Is everything OK over there? Howie acting normal?"

"I talked to her, and she says he's acting like he didn't even do anything. When she asked him about it, he played dumb. He didn't remember drinking anything at all. She's very frustrated with him. But all's well at the cafe and bowling alley."

Wilma Jean pointed at the TV, as the announcer said, "And we now have some breaking news on the Calico Callie case. Rumor on the street has it that Callie had mentioned to several close friends that she was having a serious dispute with someone over—what else —money."

As he spoke, photos of the singer in costume were displayed on the screen. Bud was impressed at the elaborate costumes Calico Callie had, and they must have cost a fortune—rhinestones and fancy cowgirl boots and such. Even though he felt bad that she'd been killed, it was kind of cool to see her in stage dress, as he could now imagine what Wilma Jean would look like if she were to ever become a famous country-western singer.

The announcer continued. "There's also some speculation that Callie's long-time manager was seen in Redstone at the time of the murder, but that seems normal to us, as he was, after all, her manager. But to make things even more interesting, our sources say Callie was seen *alive* after her body had been taken to the hospital. Let me repeat that—she was seen walking around *alive* in Redstone after she was supposedly dead. Now, I personally don't believe in zombies, but something strange is afoot."

The announcer paused, as if considering what he'd just said. "But we in no way mean to imply Callie's relatives or manager had anything to do with any of this, or that the sheriff's office is in on a fake murder. We're just repeating what the rumors are saying."

He paused, thinking, then continued. "Who knows, maybe

Callie's still alive and hoping to collect on a big insurance policy or something, though that wouldn't make sense, as she was already wealthy. But maybe someone else is hoping to collect on an insurance policy or something, though that wouldn't make sense either if she is still alive."

The announcer was now looking confused, and it was obvious someone behind the camera was signaling for him to cut, as he put his hand to his throat.

He continued, stumbling, "Actually, none of this makes sense. I personally hope she is still alive, but if she is, she might want to lie low for a bit until this all blows over. But it's time to hear from our sponsor."

The announcer was starting to remind him a little of Howie, Bud thought, shaking his head.

Wilma Jean looked irritated and said, "Spreading rumors is not what I'd call good investigative reporting."

Bud replied, "I don't think he was a real reporter, just someone doing the memorial. Maybe even an intern at the station, from the looks of him—a fairly young guy."

Wilma Jean asked, "Do you think people were mistaking me for Callie? That would explain a few things. Maybe we *should* go back to Green River. We could just stay in the back of the bowling alley until we go to Radium. Put a bed and a bit of furniture in my office there. It won't be much of a vacation here if everyone thinks I'm a zombie."

She sounded somewhat worried, which was unlike her, as she usually handled everything with aplomb. Bud had a lot of respect for his wife's intelligence, business acumen, and independence, and seeing her worried was unsettling.

"Look, hon," Bud said, "Whatever's going on here, you have nothing to worry about. Even if the police were to come and ask questions, it would soon be obvious that you have nothing to do with this. Just because someone resembles someone else doesn't mean they *are* that person or had anything to do with them."

Wilma Jean replied, "I know, but it's also impossible to prove a negative. I mean, how can I prove I'm not Calico Callie if I look just like her?"

"There are lots of ways. Dental records, fingerprints, even talking to people who knew her. Hannah knows you're not her. She said you resembled her until you got up close."

"Do you think they'll say I had anything to do with it?" Wilma Jean looked perplexed.

Bud replied, "I have no idea what's going on, but maybe I need to find out."

Bud was feeling that same sense of injustice he'd often felt when he was sheriff and someone had wronged some innocent. It hadn't happened often, but when it did, it brought out a determination that, as sheriff, his job was to make things right.

The tone of their voices had awakened Pierre, who was now looking concerned.

Wilma Jean leaned back. "Hon, let's wait a bit and see how it plays out. No need to jump the gun." She pulled Pierre up onto her lap. "Let's just deal with things as they play out."

Bud answered, "Well, a good sheriff will investigate everything, including rumors, even if they're rumors of a zombie, to see if they might have substance."

He could now see someone driving up to the cottage, and he pulled the lace curtain aside to see better.

He added, fingering the beads in his pocket, "And it looks like Pitkin County might just have a competent sheriff, because he just pulled up out front."

## 9

Bud now sat on the back veranda, the sheriff gone, watching a few wispy clouds above the canyon rim turn pink in the evening sunset. He thought of the big sweeping desert sunsets in Green River, and for a moment he was a bit homesick.

He then chided himself. How could someone be homesick when they'd only been away from home for a week? It would only be a few more weeks before he would be home again, or close to home and back in the desert, down in Radium.

Maybe it was the conversation he and Wilma Jean had had with the Pitkin Country Sheriff earlier—it made him wish for the simplicity of his little desert town.

Sheriff Mason was affable and congenial enough, but Bud hadn't felt that same sense of camaraderie he'd felt with other officers over in Utah—or anywhere, for that matter. He'd been to a couple of Utah sheriffs' conferences, and he'd clicked with most everyone he met, but this sheriff was different.

Wilma Jean had felt the same way, and she'd later said it was a cultural difference. She'd done a little Internet research on him and found he'd come from Seattle, and she attributed his work in a big city as part of what Bud was feeling.

She also pointed out that local sheriffs often reflect the personalities and values of their constituents, who, after all, vote them in, and Aspen had a good many inhabitants with urban roots.

Bud had considered her theory and what it said about Howie being sheriff of Green River, then decided to let that thought go.

Sheriff Mason hadn't seemed all that interested in Bud's role as former sheriff of Emery County. It wasn't that Bud was trying to impress him, he was simply trying to establish the fact that Wilma Jean was the wife of a former lawman, which would make her less likely to be someone suspicious, or so he figured.

But Sheriff Mason had brushed him off, asked Wilma Jean a few pertinent questions, then for permission to take her fingerprints. Wilma Jean had asked if she were a suspect or not.

The sheriff had said "probably not," then dropped the matter. He seemed unwilling to press things. He told Bud he'd thought for a minute that Wilma Jean was Calico Callie, and this had upset him. He'd then thanked them and left.

Bud wondered what the sheriff's office in a glitzy well-heeled town like Aspen had for its budget. He also wondered why the sheriff had been upset upon seeing Wilma Jean and thinking she was Callie. Surprised, yes, but why upset? Had he known Callie personally?

Bud sighed, watching the last rays of the sun turn the cliffs a deep burgundy. The dogs were with Wilma Jean, everyone napping on the couch, and Bud had put a puffy down comforter over them all, knowing it would get chilly in the night. Wilma Jean seemed to do better with her foot resting on the couch's arm, so Bud hadn't wanted to wake her to tell her to go to bed.

He tried to tip his chair back, something not amenable to heavy wicker, and instead ended up scooting it backwards, making a grating sound on the blue slate tiles.

For a moment, he expected to see the dogs, thinking he'd probably awakened them, but when they didn't show, he figured they must prefer the cozy comforter to his lap.

Bud really enjoyed the cool night air here, something that Green River had only in the early morning hours, as it took awhile for the warm desert air to cool down. Here, in the mountains, it wasn't all that hot during the day, so as soon as the sun set, things cooled quickly.

Now the cliffs were a deep purple, and it was almost pitch dark. He was tired, but kept putting off going to bed. It would be the first time he'd slept alone since his wife had taken a trip with Maureen to Salt Lake City to see the Mormon Tabernacle Choir (the "MoTab" as they were called in Utah). They'd performed with Wilma Jean's favorite singer, Nana Mouscouri.

Bud liked Mouscouri well enough, but not well enough to brave the freeway traffic up north, so had stayed home. Besides, someone had to look after the dogs.

He grinned, fingering the smooth beads in his pocket. Now, if the MoTab would do a concert with Johnny Cash, he would go, even though Johnny was now on the other side and not able to do any concerts.

He leaned back, enjoying the picture in his mind's eye of Johnny and the MoTab singing *Folsom Prison Blues*, or *I Walk the Line*, or maybe even *Ghost Riders in the Sky*, when he suddenly startled.

He swore there was something or someone standing near the bushes of the Ice House Cafe, just like the other night. Was it that darn supposed ghost thing again? This time, the dogs weren't there to verify that the shadow was real, so he had to rely on his own senses.

He sat up straight, straining to see through the darkness. Yup, sure enough, someone was there. He could see an elbow sticking out, and now it looked like they'd turned sideways and were doing something with the cafe's trash can.

Whoever it was, they didn't have that white sheen in the moonlight like the figure of the other night, probably because the moon hadn't yet risen, nor were they as thin and lithe, but were instead rather stocky.

He stood, ready to go back into the safety of the house, even though the veranda was screened in. He felt unsettled, just as he'd felt on the trail at Hays Creek Falls.

Now the person or thing had emerged from shadow and was

quickly coming straight for the cottage, though they appeared to be loping along on all fours, looking sort of like Quasimodo.

Bud was frozen for a second until his brain finally processed what was now a mere thirty feet away.

It was a bear!

# 10

Bud'd had a few run-ins with black bears when he was in high school and working summers with his grandpa out at the Preston Nutter Ranch in Nine Mile Canyon near where his grandparents lived in Price, Utah.

Bears would occasionally come down from the high country of the nearby Tavaputs Plateau, presumably to see what was on the other side of the mountain, and typically, when they saw Bud, they turned and ran, just the same as he did.

This bear either hadn't been in communication with Utah bears or else it hadn't seen Bud standing in the darkness of the veranda, because it was still coming toward him.

In any case, Bud figured it would be the better part of valor to run inside and slam the door, which he did, waking Wilma Jean. The dogs promptly started barking.

Bud wasn't sure what to do next, as he didn't think the bear would be very likely to try to break in, though he'd heard of such, especially in the autumn like this when they were trying to fatten up for hibernation and desperately looking for calories.

He heard Wilma Jean say, "What's going on, Bud?"

Bud made his way to the living room, wondering if he'd locked the front door or not. Wilma Jean was sitting up, the dogs by her side, looking at the front window. Bud turned and swore he could see the outline of the bear, and it appeared to be standing on the front step.

He replied, "There's a bear outside."

Now Wilma Jean stood up, her weight on one leg, holding onto the couch arm for support. "Maybe we should call the sheriff," she replied.

But before Bud could answer, he could now hear what sounded like a light rapping on the door.

"Hon, it's knocking on the door," Wilma Jean said as the dogs again began barking. "I don't think it would be wise to let it in. Sometimes one can be too polite."

Bud stood, frozen, then said, "Maybe I should get that pot roast from the fridge and throw it out there as a diversion."

The rapping came again, but now louder and more insistent.

Wilma Jean replied, "I don't think we should feed it. You know that saying, 'a fed bear is a dead bear.' It makes them associate people with food, which is bad."

Bud groaned, coming to his senses. "Bears can't knock on doors. They don't have hands."

"You don't need hands, all you need is knuckles."

He replied, "Don't you usually have hands if you have knuckles? Look, go into the bedroom, take the dogs, and lock the door. I'm going to see what's going on."

Bud now stealthily walked to the front door, staying away from the window, where the bear might see him.

He grabbed the door knob, ready to pull it open, when the thought of how absurd it all was hit him. He was actually thinking of opening a secure door to a bear, just so he could scare it off.

Bud paused. No matter what other foibles he might have, he had always prided himself on being pragmatic and level-headed. Opening that door was maybe the dumbest thing he'd ever contemplated doing, except maybe in another case when he'd suspected a mild-mannered chef of being a Mafioso over at a cafe near Green River.

The door was now almost shaking, as whoever was outside was pounding on it. Bud snuck a peek through the window.

What he saw now left him feeling confused. This was no bear, but rather a small woman wearing what looked to be a white leather jacket. He quickly opened the door and grabbed the woman by the arm, pulling her inside, then locking the door.

"It's nice to see we're on the same page," she said, pulling her arm away. "But why did it take you so long to answer the door?"

"There's a bear outside," he said. "And what do you mean, on the same page?"

The woman was dressed in an expensive white fringed leather jacket, a lavender silk dress, and tall white leather boots with a fringe that matched the jacket.

She held out her hand, and Bud noted she was also wearing soft white leather gloves. He tentatively shook her hand, as she answered, "I mean we're on the same page in that I wanted to come inside quickly, as I don't want anyone knowing I'm here. I didn't know there was a stupid bear out there."

She sounded like a bear was an everyday thing and nothing much to take note of.

She added, "I'm Dusty Jensen. You may know me as Calico Callie's sister, which seems to be the shadow under which I'm destined to live. Would you mind closing that curtain, and may I sit down?"

Bud was speechless. He pulled the curtain closed, wondering where the bear had gone, then replied, "Of course, but you'll get covered in dog hair."

Dusty ran her hand across the couch, then shook the hair off her glove. "No matter. Nothing's going to deter me from my mission." She sat down, her jaw set in determination.

"What mission?" Bud asked, perplexed.

"The mission to hire you to figure out who killed my sister. I'm sure you've heard the news. She was murdered. Aren't you a private investigator?"

"Me?" Bud asked, even more perplexed. "Who told you that?"

"The waitress over at the Ice House Cafe."

Just then, Wilma Jean appeared in the bedroom doorway.

"Is someone here, Bud?" she asked. "What happened to the bear?"

As Wilma Jean's eyes met Dusty's, Bud swore he could see an electrical flash as shock registered on Dusty's face.

## 11

Bud watched as Dusty drove off. It was too dark to see what kind of car she drove, but he could tell that someone had been waiting for her, as she got into the passenger side.

He pulled the curtain closed, wondering if the bear were hiding nearby. It was probably long gone on down the boulevard raiding trash cans, he figured.

Wilma Jean sat down on the couch again, putting her leg up.

Bud said, "Boy, it was something to see the look on her face. She actually thought you were Callie for a moment."

"She did seem shocked," Wilma Jean replied. "Like she thought I was a zombie or something. She looked at me the entire time, like she couldn't believe it."

Bud sat down next to her on the couch. "I can't believe she tried to give me the keys to the castle. I'm not a detective. I'm not even sure I want to take the job. What I really want to take is a vacation."

"Well, she sure wouldn't take no for an answer. And I can't believe the kind of money she was talking about. We could get that used Airstream trailer Billy Johnson has for sale and set it up as a guest cottage out in the field, like we've been talking about. I think you should sleep on it."

She then added, "And I'm kind of concerned about her wanting to keep everything hush hush."

"I think that's probably standard when one's a detective," Bud replied. "If everyone knows you're out trying to detect things, they're going to be less likely to let certain things be detectable."

"Makes sense," Wilma Jean replied, then said, "Kind of, anyway." She then scooted over next to Bud, putting her hand on his.

"Hon, let's just go home. I've had it. Murder, bears, me spraining my ankle, the sheriff acting like I'm a suspect, and now this woman wanting you to find who killed her sister, who you didn't even know. How do we know she didn't kill Callie herself and is hiring you as a way to look innocent?"

"How exactly would that work?" Bud asked.

"Well," Wilma Jean replied, "She could tell everyone she's hired a P.I. Nobody would hire a detective if they were guilty of the crime, as most detectives would figure them out."

"Not if they were some two-bit ex-sheriff from some little desert scrub town in the middle of nowhere," Bud said. "If she killed her own sister, maybe she wants to hire me because she doesn't think I'd be able to solve the crime. You're right. She can tell everyone she hired a detective, and that will make her look innocent."

"Well, she has no idea what she's in for, if that's her motive. But why don't we just leave? This isn't much fun anymore."

Bud answered, "Look, we've had a bad start, I agree, but we're supposed to be on vacation. Tell you what, I have an idea."

Bud was playing with the beads in his pocket.

"What?" she asked.

"Let's go shopping tomorrow."

"What?"

"You know, that thing you and Maureen like to do, shopping."

"Really? Are you serious? We could go to Aspen."

Bud groaned. He knew his idea would backfire on him, but he hadn't expected it to happen so quickly. Aspen was the last place he wanted to go, especially to shop.

Wilma Jean was excited. "Aspen would be fun. I know it's expensive, but we could just go window shopping, maybe buy a little souvenir or two, like a t-shirt or something. You'll have to help me hobble around."

Bud replied, "I was thinking more along the lines of maybe just visiting some of the shops here along the boulevard or going someplace down valley, like Carbondale, or even Glenwood Springs. Glenwood looked like it had lots of nice shops, and it's closer."

"You do realize that the term 'down valley' is how the Aspenites refer to everywhere else—sometimes derogatively, since everywhere else is down valley from them?"

"Well, I'm more of a down valley kind of guy myself," Bud replied. "But I guess we can go to Aspen if you want. I'm going to go have a bowl of ice cream, then go to bed. All this excitement's drained my energy levels."

"You need energy to sleep?"

"No, but I have just enough energy to get into the kitchen but not to the bedroom, as it's too far, and there's no way you can help me with your ankle like that."

Bud stood and headed for the kitchen, the dogs trailing behind. They'd been all cozy by Wilma Jean on the couch, but now figured that following Bud into the kitchen might be worthwhile.

Just then, Wilma Jean's phone rang. Bud could hear her talking as he took the vanilla-bean ice cream from the freezer and put a few scoops into a bowl, then gave Hoppie and Pierre each a little bite around the kitchen corner where he wouldn't be seen. He walked back into the living room as she hung up.

"That was Maureen," Wilma Jean reported. "Howie still hasn't shown up from work. He's usually home by 5:30 and it's 10:30. He hasn't called or anything. She's worried sick."

"And she can't call the sheriff," Bud added. "Because he *is* the sheriff and isn't answering his phone."

Bud sat down by Wilma Jean. "If he doesn't show up, I'll take the train over and see what's going on."

"Hon, if you leave, I'll be stuck here. I can't drive with my ankle like this," Wilma Jean replied. "I can't even take the dogs out. In fact, I can't even take you to the train station."

"Shoots, I forgot. Well, it looks like Howie's on his own," Bud replied grimly. "Or else I'll have to take the Lincoln and you guys with me. You've been wanting to go home. Maybe we should just go."

"Well, let's wait and see what the morning brings. What's Hoppie eating? Ice cream? Bud?"

Bud groaned as Hoppie licked ice cream from his paw, where he'd apparently dropped the bite Bud had given him. Bud soon tucked everyone in and headed off to bed, tired.

That night, he dreamed that a big black bear broke down the door and stormed into the cottage, only to turn into Dusty Jensen, who stood looking at Bud, holding the keys to the Redstone Castle in one hand and a very expensive bowl of ice cream in the other.

# 12

Bud woke early and was soon up, making a pot of percolator coffee. Wilma Jean and the dogs were already sitting out on the veranda, Wilma Jean drinking tea.

Bud fed the dogs, took them outside for a bit down by the river, then made himself and Wilma Jean a breakfast of scrambled eggs and toast.

Wilma Jean hadn't called Maureen yet, so Bud decided to see if he could get ahold of Howie and make sure he'd come home, as well as try to find out where he'd been.

He hoped Howie hadn't been drinking again, but had an unsettled feeling that maybe he had. If so, he knew Howie's career as Sheriff of Emery County could easily be coming to a close, technically before it had officially even started, as the election was still a few weeks off, in early November.

Even though Howie was now sheriff, he hadn't been voted in, but rather, as Bud's deputy, had gotten the office by default when Bud quit. The election would be a test of what the people of Emery County thought of Howie's handling of the duties of sheriff.

Bud dialed Howie's cell phone, then waited as it rang, holding his breath a bit.

"Sheriff Howie here," Howie answered.

Bud let out his breath, realizing how worried he'd been.

"Howie, everything OK?"

"Oh hey, Sheriff, nice to hear from you. Sure, everything's fine. Pretty quiet around here these days. I'm sure you noticed I didn't even call you yesterday."

Howie paused, then added, "Actually, now that I think of it, we did have some excitement yesterday evening. The Hazmat team from Price came down."

"Oh?" Bud replied, then sat down on the couch and waited, picking up an old copy of *National Geographic*.

Finally, after Bud had become engrossed in an article about the language of the African Hottentots and how they use clicks for consonants, Howie finally continued.

"Well, Bud, you know old Charlie Litfin, well he was down at the ballpark letting off steam and somebody got worried and called the State Patrol, and they called in the Hazmat guys. I guess they tried to call me, but I think it was when I was out taking a walk, because I didn't hear the phone ring."

"They called the Hazmat for somebody letting off steam? What was he doing, yelling or something?"

"Yelling? Nah, he's that guy they call Thunder Dog, you know, he drives that big nitrogen truck, lives a block from the old ball field and parks his rig there. He was letting off pressure from the truck. I guess those nitrogen trucks need that, but it's not dangerous. I called him this morning, and he said that the air we breathe is 78 percent nitrogen, nothing dangerous about it. I guess we're breathing the stuff all the time, though I thought we were more into oxygen, but apparently not."

Bud put the magazine down. "Well, I'm glad that turned out OK. But Howie, Maureen called last night, and we were all pretty worried about you."

"Yeah, I sure feel bad about that. I bought Maureen some flowers down at Dwaine's hardware store."

"Flowers from the hardware store?"

"Yeah, you know, he sells garden stuff. I got her a nice potted plant —I think it was a tomato or something—and some potted petunias."

"But Howie, is everything OK? It's really none of my business, but don't you think the sheriff maybe should be pretty careful about what he does on his own hours?"

Howie replied, "You mean our band practice? Howie and the Ramblin' Road Rangers?"

"Well, no, not unless something else is going on..."

"Well, Sheriff, I agree, the sheriff has to set a good example. We haven't been practicing like we should, I admit."

Bud groaned to himself, then asked, "Well, so you've been going home at night and all that? Not out doing anything you shouldn't?"

"Well, Sheriff, not that I know of. I came in late last night because I had to walk home. It was a bit of a hike."

"Why did you have to walk home?"

"Because the old Crown Vic broke down."

"Broke down? Where?"

Howie replied, "Well, Sheriff, I've been real worried about the stolen Land Cruiser, and I've been out cruising around some of the back roads in case somebody took it out joy riding then left it someplace."

Howie paused for a moment, and Bud was about to pick up the magazine again when he continued.

"I was way out by that dinosaur quarry by the geyser when I hit a bump kind of hard. I looked back behind me and saw something in the road. So, I got out and looked. It was the drive shaft off some-body's vehicle. When I got back into the Crown Vic and started back up, I realized that vehicle was mine."

"You were way out there? That's probably 10 miles from town, Howie. Why didn't you call someone to come and get you?"

"No cell service, and by the time I got back to where I could use my phone, it was late and I didn't want to wake anyone up, so I just walked home. Man, I'm sore today."

"I bet. Howie, call the Mayor and tell him your office wants to lease my FJ. The keys are in the drawer under the microwave. They used to lease my old Bronco before we got the Land Cruiser, so I know he'll be OK with it. Is anyone dealing with the Crown Vic?"

"Yeah, I called Desert Rescue Towing. They're going to get it today and take it to the shop."

"Good," Bud replied. He felt a bit easier, knowing Howie hadn't come in late because he'd been drinking. He added, "Howie, are you feeling pretty stressed? Is there anything I can help with?"

"Stressed?" Howie replied. "Nah, Sheriff, I'm fine. Like I said, not all that much going on. Some guy called this morning to report somebody had stolen the seat off his bicycle, but other than that, it's real quiet."

"Where was the seat?"

"Attached to his bicycle, on top of his car. Some guy heading home from Radium. He actually called it a saddle, not a seat. Said it was carbon fiber, plated with rhodium and made by somebody called Crown and cost almost $1500. Bud, that seat cost two times more than my recliner, and I bet my recliner's a lot more comfortable."

Bud laughed. "OK, Howie, I hope he finds it. But you be sure to call me if you need anything, and I don't care how minor it may be, just call me."

"Roger, Sheriff, you know I will," Howie replied, and hung up.

# 13

Sheriff Mason sat somewhat stiffly behind his desk, running his fingers through his graying hair, a bronze nameplate announcing to the world that he was Sheriff of Pitkin County, Colorado. Only those not in the know didn't equate Pitkin County to the tony town of Aspen.

Finally, he said, "Well, Mr. Shumway, I can't say I understand why you're here. Maybe you could elucidate that a bit."

Bud was glad he was on the non-business side of that desk, having spent a number of years himself on the business side of a similar one.

He'd decided to go ahead and bring Wilma Jean to Aspen to shop. He'd found her a pair of crutches in a second-hand store in Carbondale on the way up, and last he saw, she was happily hopping her way down Main Street, the dogs sleeping in the car. They would meet up in an hour, as he had a little business here with the sheriff he wanted to do.

Bud dug into the pocket of his khaki pants, pulling out the strand of beads from his great aunt, then offered them to the sheriff.

"Here, you can borrow these for awhile."

"What?" Sheriff Mason looked startled. "What is it?"

"It's what I use when I need to fiddle. See, Sheriff, I can't think without fiddling, and the way you keep tapping your fingers and running them through your hair, I suspect we're partners in crime that way."

The sheriff looked irritated.

"Look, Sheriff Mason," Bud continued, putting the beads back in his pocket, "We're both part of the thin blue line, even though I'm no longer a law officer. Our techniques may differ, but we're both interested in seeing bad guys brought to justice. Am I right?"

Bud knew he was putting Sheriff Mason on the spot, making him condescend to admit they were colleagues, even though he suspected that Mason considered him a hick.

"Say," Bud continued. "Do you even know where Green River, Utah is? Do you have a map handy? Pull up one on your computer there—MapQuest or Google Maps or something like that."

Bud was sure the sheriff had figured they didn't even use computers over in Podunk, Utah and would be surprised Bud knew anything about such.

He continued, "Use your search bar there and key in Green River, Utah. There's one in Wyoming, too, so don't get them confused. Best melons in the world. Some real beautiful wild country, too, over 4,462 square miles with a population of under 10,000. I had only one under-trained deputy to help out."

Now Sheriff Mason stood, visibly irritated.

"Mr. Shumway..."

"Call me Bud."

"OK, um, Bud, you know I can't tell you anything about Calico Callie's murder. If you really were sheriff over there, you know that's against the rules. We can't release any evidence to anyone not actively involved in the case."

"But I *am* actively involved," Bud replied. "Just not officially."

"Why are you so interested in this case?" Mason's eyes narrowed as he sat back down.

"I'm considering whether or not to hire on as a private investigator."

"Who wants to hire you?"

"That's confidential."

Sheriff Mason looked even more irritated, stood up again, and started pacing behind his desk.

"I think I can guess who it might be, and I'll just warn you that she is currently one of our suspects. Are you licensed?" he asked Bud.

"Colorado doesn't require one," Bud replied.

"OK, I knew that," Sheriff Mason answered testily, as if Bud had caught him in a lapse. He continued. "Look, this is a very high-profile case. Our reputation is on the line. We have a number of famous people here who are beginning to wonder if they're still safe."

Bud replied, "Sheriff, there's a major mountain range between Redstone and Aspen, as the crow flies, and they're an hour apart by highway, even though it's only about 45 miles. It's a slow drive because of the canyon. Why would your constituents worry about a murder in Redstone?"

Sheriff Mason sat back down. "Calico Callie was one of their own, a celebrity. The murderer could be someone nuts who's looking to make a reputation for themselves, or it could be the result of some kind of blackmail. Any of these things could affect someone rich and famous. You wouldn't believe some of the crazy things we've had happen here. And Callie was pretty darn famous—and rich."

"Why are you considering my wife to be a suspect?" Bud decided to throw the question out, hoping to catch the sheriff off guard.

Now the sheriff stood again, then sat back down and tipped his chair back, tapping his fingers on the desktop. "Your wife's not a suspect. It was just procedural. Someone said she was Callie in hiding, and we had to do our duty and check it out."

Bud replied, "That's the other reason I want this private-eye job, is for my wife's peace of mind. If I take it on, will you guys work with me?" Bud asked, knowing full well they probably wouldn't.

"I can't say we would," Sheriff Mason replied. "But give me some references, and I'll look into it. I would hope, however, that you would let us in on anything you might find, even though I probably can't offer you the same courtesy."

Just then, someone knocked on the door.

"Come in."

A tall thin deputy entered, nodded hello at Bud, then said, "Sheriff, we're still having problems over at Jack Nicholson's old house there in the West End. I have an officer over there standing by. They're trying to tear the old shed down."

Sheriff Mason replied, "Did someone call us? That's the jurisdiction of the town police, Arnie. Why are we over there?"

"The police are busy with traffic control for that big wedding up in Starwood, plus they just arrested a bunch of Defeat the Elite protestors at the street mall, so they called us. The guy's trying to tear the shed down, even though his permit says he can't. He's threatening to sue. What should we do?"

"I guess I'd better go on over there," he replied. "That's the house Nicholson bought because he couldn't get reception for the Lakers games over where he lived in the Maroon Creek subdivision. He would go over to this house just to watch the games. It's on the Historic Register, and this new buyer wants to tear everything up or down, whatever he thinks he can get away with."

Sheriff Mason stood, shook Bud's hand, then as they both walked out the door, he added, "See what I mean about crazy? It's hard to get any real work done around here. We employ 25 deputies to patrol approximately 1,000 square miles, or roughly the size of the State of Rhode Island, much of which is mountainous. I do know where Green River is, and I can't believe you had only one deputy to help you cover 4,462 square miles of desert wilderness. You have my ongoing admiration."

The sheriff stopped, rubbing his nose as he thought, then added, "We'll work with you as best we can, but don't expect much. And beads really do work, huh?"

Bud grinned as they walked out the courthouse door. He had no illusions that he would be privy to confidential information, but Sheriff Mason hadn't been quite as off-putting as he'd thought he would be.

Maybe things would work out after all, but he had some thinking to do before he decided whether or not to go to work for someone the sheriff considered to be a murder suspect.

# 14

Bud sat in the back booth in the Ice House Cafe, drinking coffee and looking at the big ice tongs on the wall above his booth, hoping they were well-anchored. Wilma Jean and the dogs were taking a nap over at the cottage.

It had now been a couple of days since their trip to Aspen, and his wife's ankle seemed to be healing fine, though she was still taking it easy.

Earlier that morning, they'd visited the coke ovens across the highway from Redstone, a historic site with a placard telling how the large red-brick beehive ovens were built for making coke, which was used by nearby silver and gold smelters. The area near Redstone held some of the best bituminous coal in the world, known for its purity and low ash content.

Bud had enjoyed learning more about the history of Redstone, but for now, his attentions were on his computer screen, where he was reading the detective report for the murder of Callie Jensen, AKA Calico Callie.

He'd come to the cafe to use the wifi after Sheriff Mason had called him, telling him his references had checked out and he was going to share the information they had so far on the case, though it was to be considered strictly confidential. Bud knew Sheriff Mason had his hands full and was probably hoping Bud could help them out.

Callie's wing of the castle had been ordered closed, but nobody had been able to get back down to check it out, with all the mayhem going on in Aspen, including a major landslide on Independence Pass, which had closed down the highway going out that direction. And they'd been especially short-handed, as one of their deputies had quit to become a private guard at twice the pay for some celebrity.

Bud could understand why a deputy would switch jobs like that. He'd been tempted to take up Dusty Jensen's offer to work for her, but he just didn't know enough about her. She'd been disappointed when he'd called to tell her he couldn't go to work for her. She'd then upped the ante by offering him even more money.

Bud had hesitated, thinking of how much Wilma Jean wanted that Airstream trailer as a guesthouse, but even that wasn't enough to entice him to work for someone he didn't feel comfortable with. Plus, Dusty was such a bulldog, he suspected he wouldn't be allowed to do things his way and there would be constant battles. And then there was the matter of Sheriff Mason saying she was a suspect.

But Dusty was apparently used to getting things her way, and Bud had finally told her he was going to solve the case on his own, basically working for himself. When she'd asked if he was able to pay himself what she had offered, he'd told her she could write him a check if he was able to solve the case, and then only if she was so inclined.

Being stubborn, she'd then wanted him to sign a contract, but he'd refused, saying he had no intention of answering to her or anyone else. That had finally made his point, and she'd hung up.

Bud was now riveted to the report the sheriff had emailed him, as it was the first real information he'd had on the murder. All he knew was what the TV had reported, which matched what Hannah the waitress had told them—that Callie had been found on the grounds near her bedroom. No one had said how she'd been killed, but now Bud knew.

According to the report, a muffled and very excited voice had called 911 and reported finding her body. When asked who was calling, the voice had simply said Juneau Alaska, and this had confused the 911 operator, who then thought the crime was in Juneau and proceeded to try to somehow connect with the Juneau police, putting the caller on hold for some time.

Bud was now confused himself, but he kept reading. Apparently, the caller told the 911 dispatcher that he had seen blood on the victim's forehead, though his voice was so muffled and low she could barely understand him.

Finally, after asking a half dozen times where the body was located, the dispatcher sent out a sheriff's deputy, who arrived to find Callie's body near the deck off her bedroom. Whoever had called in the crime had disappeared, and the sheriff's office was still trying to track down the cell phone owner, which was tricky, as it was a prepaid phone from Walmart.

Further investigation revealed that Callie had died instantly from a heavy blow to her forehead, cracking her skull. The coroner reported that whatever had been used to kill her had to be somewhat heavy and metal with an end that tapered to a sharp point, like a rock hammer.

The sheriff's office had found no nearby tracks and no clues. The rest of the report consisted of interviews with various friends of Callie in Aspen, as well as with her sister, Dusty. None revealed anything of note.

Bud quickly switched on his screen saver, a photo of a train, as Hannah came to refill his coffee cup. He was still leery of her and wondering what she'd been up to that day at Hays Creek Falls.

She'd acted happy to see him when he came into the cafe today, like nothing at all was different, so he'd let down his guard a little, but there was no way he would risk her seeing what he was reading.

Hannah stood over him, angled where she could see his screen, and refilling his cup, said, "That's a very cool photo. Where was it taken?"

"Over by Green River," Bud replied. "I won grand champ in an art show with it."

He suddenly felt like he was bragging and changed the subject. "Say, you guys have vanilla ice cream? Could I have a small scoop to add to my coffee? Sort of an old habit I got myself into when I was on a special diet."

"What kind of diet lets you eat ice cream?" Hannah replied. "Sounds like one I could stick to for once."

"It's a special diet I came up with myself. All the ice cream you want, but you have to eat salads the rest of the time."

"Did it work?" Hannah asked.

"Well, you're looking at the results," Bud replied, patting where his stomach pushed a bit over his belt. "But I have to admit I didn't test it for very long. I ran out of ice cream in the first couple of days, even though I'd stocked up on several gallons. And that was about when my wife found out about it and shut it down."

Hannah smiled and was soon back with a small dish of ice cream. She sat down opposite Bud as he put a dollop into his coffee.

"Say," she asked, "You mind telling me why you guys are over here? I know it's none of my business, but I can't help but notice the sheriff visited you, and you sure seem to run around a lot. And then your wife gets injured somehow, and with her looking like she could be Calico Callie's twin sister, and then Callie's *real* sister coming to visit you..."

"Well," Bud replied, "We're really just here on vacation, hard as that is to believe. But how did you know Dusty came to visit?" Bud was annoyed at her nosiness, but tried not to show it.

"I live up there," Hannah pointed to the ceiling of the cafe. "I can see everything that happens in Redstone from my windows because I'm up high. I'm not nosy, I just like to sit and look out. I get seriously claustrophobic, especially at night. By the way, there was a bear messing around your place the other night, just before Callie's sister visited you. The D.O.W. was here yesterday, and they're going to trap and relocate it."

"What's the D.O.W.?" Bud asked.

"Department of Wildlife."

"Oh sure, I should've guessed," he said. "We call it the D.W.R. over in Utah, Department of Wildlife Resources."

Just then, a small group of motorcyclists with leather jackets wearing emblems that read, "Minot Marauders" came into the cafe. Hannah stood to go, then added, "And that ghost was seen again just last night."

"Did you see it?" Bud asked, eyeing the bikers, a couple of them looking vaguely familiar.

"Heaven forbid I ever see that weird thing," she replied. "No, it was seen by one of the kids who lives down the street. His mom came in this morning and told me about it. It was trying to look into your windows. Be mighty careful today, my friend."

With that, Hannah was gone, waiting on the biker bunch.

## 15

Bud was on the grounds of the Redstone Castle, down on his hands and knees, examining the area where Calico Callie had been found, according to the map that was attached to the report he'd received from Sheriff Mason.

So far, he hadn't found anything of note, except a small piece of metal that appeared to have fallen from the edge of the castle's metal gutters high above, gutters that looked like they could use a good painting of Rustoleum. It was hard to really be thorough, as the vegetation here by the deck off Callie's bedroom was thick and overgrown.

Bud had done some gravity tests a few minutes before while up on the deck, throwing a couple of heavy patio chairs off, then gently pushing off a couple more, just to see where they would fall.

From this, he'd deduced that Callie had probably been thrown from the deck, as her body was out farther than it would be if she'd merely fallen. Odds were thereby good that she'd been killed by someone *before* falling.

At first, he'd wondered if maybe the fall hadn't killed her, as the deck was a good 10 feet off the ground, but the coroner's report had said otherwise, that she'd been killed by a blow to the head with a heavy sharp object, not from the fall.

But what if she'd been thrown off and consequently landed on something hard and sharp? Bud figured that could possibly mimic a blow to the head. But if so, where was the object she'd fallen onto? The report hadn't mentioned anything.

Bud himself hadn't found a thing, as the piece of metal he'd just found was too small to 'cause the wound, and as he stood, brushing the black loamy soil from his pants, he noticed a nearby shadow that hadn't been there when he knelt down.

He turned to find a short stocky guy looking at him, then realized it was the same fellow he'd seen with Hannah up at Hays Creek Falls. The man held a shovel, and the look on his face told Bud he might be on the receiving end of it if he didn't watch his P's and Q's, whatever that meant.

"Afternoon," Bud offered, noting the guy was going bald, even though he had a thick dark beard.

"Afternoon," the fellow returned, though not very cordially. "You trespass often, or is this just a one time thing?"

"Trespass?" Bud asked somewhat innocently. "Nope, don't mean to trespass. You live here?"

"I'm the one doing the questioning, and yes, I live here. I'm the caretaker and groundskeeper."

Bud nodded his head knowingly. "Well, you missed this spot here. Kind of a bit of a jungle with these chokecherries growing up everywhere."

The man looked defensive. "Who are you, an investigator?"

"An investigator?" Bud was surprised at how astute the man seemed to be. "What would I be investigating?"

"You tell me."

"I'm a melon farmer. Name's Bud Shumway."

Bud held out his hand, but the fellow ignored it.

The man replied, "Oh? I'm a bit of a gardener myself. What kind of melons do you grow?"

Bud knew the guy was testing him, but he figured he could outgun about anyone in the melon department, except maybe a few old-time Green River growers like Larry Digham.

Bud replied, "Jubilee and Yellow Babies, mostly, but we've been trying out that new strain of Israeli Galias. Had a pretty good crop this year, if I don't say so myself."

He smiled, thinking of how pleased his employer, Professor Krider, had been upon seeing how much Bud had made at the Grand Junction Farmers' Market.

The man blanched a little, then tightened his grip on his shovel handle, as if afraid Bud might make a sudden move and take it from him.

Bud added, "I'm here checking out the dirt."

It was true, though maybe a bit disingenuous.

"Why the interest in the dirt *here*?" the man asked.

"Because it's such a good grower. I couldn't help but notice how nice the grounds were from the road over there, and I just had to stop by and see what I could see."

"Oh? Then why were you throwing chairs off the deck?"

"Oh, that's an old dirt compression test I learned from my grand-daddy. He was one of the best. You see, you get a feel for the weight of the chair, then you know that gravitational forces are f=mg, you throw the chair with a force of about 15 pounds or 8 kg, then measure how deep the ruts are where it landed. You can actually calculate how well the soil compacts, which is really important when you want to grow stuff."

Bud was stretching a bit, hoping he'd remembered the formula correctly from his high school days. He then added, "But any gardener worth his salt knows that, so I'm sure that's old hat to you." He looked knowingly at the man. "By the way, I didn't catch your name."

The man still looked skeptical, but now seemed unsure of himself. "Name's Juno Alaska. I grew up in Juneau, Alaska, which probably seems pretty obvious. Spell it J-U-N-O."

"That's your real name?"

"Yup. My real name, ever since I changed it."

Bud paused, thinking of the 911 call. He now knew it had to be

Juno who had called it in, but of course, there was no way a dispatcher in Aspen would know that Juno was his name.

"Why do you spell it different from the spelling of the town, Juneau?"

"That's the French spelling. Mine's the better way to spell it, not so confusing. Easier."

Bud noted that the man's grip on the shovel handle had relaxed. He tried again, holding out his hand.

"Bud Shumway. Green River, Utah. My wife and I are here on vacation."

He knew Juno already knew this, being Hannah's friend, but added it for the sake of politeness. He then remembered he had a few business cards Professor Krider had made up for him, just in case. He took one from the wallet in his pocket and handed it to Juno.

Juno looked at it, then sat down the shovel and shook Bud's hand, though hesitantly.

"You're not an investigator?"

"You're thinking of Callie, aren't you?" Bud dodged. "Everyone knows about that. What a shame. She was your employer, I take it."

"She was. I miss her. I loved her like a sister."

Juno looked sad all of a sudden, then recomposed himself, again suspicious, and said, "I'm still not convinced you're not here snooping around, trying to find something out. FBI?"

"Nope."

"IRS?"

"Nope. Was she in trouble with the IRS?" Bud asked.

"Not that I know of. Callie was as honest as the day is long and would never cheat anyone, not even the IRS, which I wish I could say about myself."

"You don't pay your taxes?"

"Don't make enough to have to. I get free housing as part of the deal, but I don't report it, if you call that cheating. I bet you're from the CIA," replied Juno.

"Nope. Why would the CIA be in Redstone?"

"They probably wouldn't."

Juno now got suddenly quiet and began fiddling with his beard. Bud was encouraged. That now made two fiddlers he'd met in just a couple of days—he wasn't the only one.

Juno added, quietly, "Now I get it. You're with the EPA. Makes sense they would send in someone who knows all that science stuff about dirt, seeing how Callie had grubstaked old Gus Dearhammer, even though I told her not to. He was working that damn silver mine and that kind of stuff always messes up the dirt."

Juno looked defeated. He picked the shovel back up and turned to go, then added, "Guess I better start job hunting. Look around all you want. You won't find nuthin'."

Bud stood for a moment, surprised by the man's about face, then started walking back to the car, wondering yet again why he'd felt so uncertain about Juno and Hannah out at the trail to Hays Creek Falls.

# 16

Bud stood behind a small tree, trying not to be too obvious as he took off his tight suit jacket so he could reach an itchy spot on his back. He replaced the jacket, but the itch started in again, so he finally just draped the jacket over a nearby chair and let it be. He would pick it up later, when Calico Callie's memorial service was over.

He'd rented the suit in the nearby town of Glenwood Springs, and it was way too tight, though it was supposedly the size he wore. He figured it must've been made in China or Pakistan or someplace where the people were a bit smaller, even though the tag inside the collar said "Made in the U.S.A." Bud guessed that, like the word "natural," the word "made" could have various meanings, one maybe being "assembled." It just couldn't be his real size.

In any case, he now knew how Pierre and Hoppie must feel when they couldn't reach an itch on their backs and started going in circles, one back leg trying to scratch and the other hopping along, until Bud or Wilma Jean would take pity and scratch them.

He wished Wilma Jean were here right now to do him a similar favor, but she had declined to come along, saying she'd never met Callie and wasn't up to being mistaken for her zombie. Bud could certainly understand that, as he himself was getting lots of looks from people who seemed to be wondering who he was, making him feel even more self-conscious in his tight suit.

The memorial service was being held on the grounds of the Redstone Inn, which set at the end of the boulevard like "a jewel on a crown," or so the marketing hype on the town's website had claimed, obviously playing on the Ruby of the Rockies theme. Even though the grounds were extensive, they were already crowded with Callie's fans and friends and a few who Bud suspected were "funeral hoppers." This was what Wilma Jean called the folks who went to everyone's memorial service or funeral, whether they had known them or not.

In Green River, these folks tended to be more elderly, and Bud postulated they might be getting a bit concerned about their own longevity and wanting to check things out. A few of these old-timers would even invite themselves to the funeral dinners, which were usually reserved for family and close friends only. Green Riverites were typically a tolerant lot, so nobody would ever say anything.

Bud had come to Callie's memorial strictly in the capacity of detective, as he wanted to check everyone out and see what he could see, but he hadn't anticipated this large of a crowd to have to check out.

There was no way he could listen in on the myriad conversations going on around him, so he resigned himself to just hanging back and observing, hoping something would possibly give him some direction in his investigation, which, so far seemed to be going nowhere.

While leaning against that same small tree, kind of using it like a cow would use a fencepost for a scratching post, Bud began to think about Callie's murder.

Bud knew that murders of passion, as they were called, were often prosecuted differently from premeditated murders. It was the premeditation part that made something a first-degree murder, the cold-blooded type, as opposed to the second degree, or "lost temper" kind of murder.

Neither types of murder were committed by sane people, and Bud knew that a sane person would never show his or her face again in any context that might help convict them of their crime—especially since, in Colorado, one could get up to 32 years for even a second-degree murder or "heat of passion" charge. A sane person would hide out and keep as low a profile as possible after murdering someone.

But murderers weren't sane, and it was very possible that Callie's murderer could show at the memorial.

Bud knew he wasn't qualified to guess about the complex psychological reasons that would drive such behavior, but he did know that sometimes a murderer became obsessed with getting caught and had to check out every situation were they might be implicated, often leading to the very thing they most feared—getting caught.

Bud noticed a man leaning over against the wall of the inn. It took a minute to figure out why the man looked so familiar, but he finally realized he was looking at Juno Alaska. Bud nodded at him, but Juno either didn't see him or ignored him.

Juno wore a camel-tan leisure suit that looked to be right out of the 70s, so well-preserved it looked brand new. He must wear it only for rare special occasions, Bud figured, noting that the pant legs were a bit too short, revealing white socks and rubber sandals made from old tires like Bud once saw at a market in Mexico.

He and Wilma Jean had gone down to Nogales once right after they'd been married, and he'd checked out a similar pair, but had decided he wasn't crazy about leaving tread marks that said "Goodyear" everywhere he walked.

Now Bud spied Dusty Jensen over by a stone-lined bed of orange and white calla lilies, dressed in what looked like pale-green silk pajamas and talking to a tall thin man in a dark-blue expensive-looking suit. The only time Bud had ever seen a suit that well-tailored was when he'd gone to a sheriffs' convention up in Salt Lake City and a state politician had given the opening talk.

The man with Dusty was wearing a bold red tie with what Bud thought might be a tie tack fishing lure—maybe a jitterbug, as it had the same shape and color. Bud knew jitterbug lures because his granddad had used them for bass fishing in the Colorado River there by Radium, and the lures were usually a bright yellow with black spots on them, kind of resembling a chubby little fish.

As Bud inched his way closer to Dusty, he could see that Juno was now across the courtyard talking to Hannah. Bud changed course, heading toward Hannah, but Dusty had spied Bud and was insistently signaling for him to come her way.

Bud changed course again and was soon next to Dusty. She put her arm around him and said, "Bud, I'd like you to meet Callie's business manager, Gene Simpson. Gene, this is Bud Shumway. He's the private detective I wanted to work for me on the case, but he declined so he could do it his way."

Gene shook hands with Bud, who verified it was indeed a jitterbug on the man's tie.

"You a fly fisherman?" asked Gene, noting Bud's interest and ignoring what Dusty had said.

"No, but I know a jitterbug when I see it," Bud grinned. "The lure of choice for bass fishing. But where do you bass fish around here?"

"Reudi Reservoir, just up the road," replied Gene. "It's where the Aspen Yacht Club hangs out. Pretty good for..."

Dusty interrupted, irritated, "See that seedy character over there?" She pointed to Juno. "I really think he had something to do with Callie's murder."

Bud was surprised. Juno now seemed to be agitated, from the way he was talking with his hands and the serious look on Hanna's face.

Dusty added, "How could any respectable parent name a kid after a city and state—Juneau Alaska—assuming that's his real name? And he's illiterate—can't even spell it correctly. Anyway, the night that Callie's body was found, I got a strange call. I finally figured out it was him—he sounded a bit drunk. He told me he'd seen blood on Callie's forehead."

Dusty stopped, as if assessing the situation, then said, "What I want to know is how could he possibly see blood on her forehead when she was lying face down? Answer me that. I fired him about an hour ago and told him to never set foot on my property again."

She seemed extremely angry, and Bud noted her hands were shaking.

Dusty then turned to Bud and said, "And I hope you're taking notes, Mr. I Work Only For Myself Private Investigator."

## 17

"Bud Shumway, remember when you left my antique peacock glass in the grass at the park? You promised to try to not be so absent minded after that."

Wilma Jean was reminding Bud very much of his mom, who, rest her soul, he would rather not remember like this.

Wilma Jean continued, "And now we have to go back to the inn and see if someone turned in your suit jacket—the one that's rented and that we'll have to pay for if we can't find."

Bud was happy to see his wife was feeling better, her ankle not bothering her much now. He wished he could figure out how not to annoy her so much, as he knew she'd then feel even better.

"I'm not your mom," she added, making sure he hadn't had a sudden memory lapse.

"I'll run over there right now," Bud replied with chagrin. "I had too much on my mind, meeting Callie's business manager, who was telling me all about how she had a reputation for not keeping track of money. She just spent it whenever and wherever and had people who made it all work, mostly him."

Wilma Jean replied, "Sounds like she wasn't in it for the money, but was instead in it for the *spending* of the money."

"Something like that," Bud said, heading out the door.

He decided to first stop at the Ice House Cafe and grab a quick cup of coffee. Sure, Bud thought a bit guiltily, they had coffee at the cottage, but it didn't come with a dollop of vanilla-bean ice cream, like it did at the cafe.

Besides, he wanted to check in with Hannah and see if she would mention anything about Juno getting fired. He knew he could count on her to be straightforward, which was another way of saying he knew she would spill whatever beans she might have.

"Morning, Hannah," Bud said as he walked in the door. A pair of road bikers sat in the back booth, eating breakfast, dressed in nylon tights and jackets, their bikes parked in front of the cafe.

"Coffee?" she asked.

"Yeah, and..."

Hannah interrupted, "I know, ice cream."

Bud grinned and sat down by the front door. Hannah was soon back with his coffee and a small dish of vanilla ice cream, sitting down in the booth opposite him.

"EPA, huh?" Hannah got right to the point.

"No, I'm a melon farmer," Bud replied. "That was something Juno made up."

"Is it true?"

"That I'm with the EPA? No. That I'm a melon farmer? Yes."

Hannah looked at him for a moment, than said, "We saw you hanging out with Dusty, Callie's sister. Did she tell you she fired Juno? After all these years working for Callie, always being there, just like that, fired. I'm sure you can guess what he thinks of that."

"Doesn't sound very fair to me," Bud replied, sipping coffee.

"Are you and her on good terms?" Hannah asked.

"We're not on any kind of terms," Bud answered.

"Then how do you know her? I told you I saw her come visit you guys that one night. Don't tell me you're not buddies. Or are you working for her somehow?"

"Not working for her, Hannah, nor anyone else. I'm on vacation."

"Juno said you were out at the castle throwing chairs off the deck. Temper tantrum?"

Bud sighed. "Look, Hannah, do you know why Dusty fired Juno?"

"No."

"He told her he'd seen blood on Callie's forehead. The only way he could've seen blood on her was if he'd been involved somehow in her murder. She was thrown off the deck after being hit by something and landed on her face. No way he could've seen her face after the fact without disturbing her body—unless he was the one that murdered her and had seen her before he threw her off."

Hannah looked shocked. "Juno? Murder? Never in a million years. We're talking about the guy who rescued a baby robin from a downed nest and fed it every half-hour for weeks until it could fly. Every half-hour! He has a heart of gold."

"Some people love animals and hate people," Bud replied. "Look, you're always asking me questions, now it's my turn. Are you and Juno friends?"

"Friends? Me and Juno? No, he's my ex-brother-in-law."

"Ex?"

"Yeah, he was married to my sister. Twenty years ago. He worked at the castle even back then, way before Callie bought it. It belonged to some newspaper publisher. He kind of goes with the castle, that's why it's such a shock for him to get fired."

Hannah leaned back. "My sis thought he was cute, and she was infatuated with the idea of getting to live at the castle. It didn't last long, as he's too quirky. But he still comes to me sometimes with his problems. I guess you could say we're friends, sort of, though I mostly feel kind of sorry for him."

"He never indicated he might be on the outs with Callie or anything like that?"

"No, he admired Callie and thought it was way cool that he worked for someone famous. He kind of liked being the guy who kept the grounds so nice."

"Was he the one who found her?"

"He said he was."

"Did he say anything to you later, like he'd somehow turned her body over? The sheriff found no tracks nearby, that's why they think she was thrown off the deck after being hit. He's implicated pretty strongly if he saw blood on her forehead."

"You are some kind of investigator, aren't you?" Hannah asked suspiciously.

"In a way, yes, but I don't work for anyone, not even the EPA. I just want to see Callie's murderer brought to justice."

"But you didn't even know her."

"Doesn't matter. Don't you feel the same way?" Bud studied Hannah, who now had a look of defeat on her face.

She replied, "Well, yes, unless..." She paused, then finally finished her sentence, "...unless it's Juno."

"What's he going to do now?" Bud asked.

"I don't know," Hannah replied. "She literally threw him out on the street, after working there some 25 years. Can you imagine that? She doesn't even know where the sprinkler heads are. Callie would never have done that."

Just then, a customer came in, and Hannah stood to go.

Bud said, "Hannah, if you hear anything about all this, let me know. I want to see Juno get his job back, and that's not going to happen until we can prove him innocent, assuming he is. Dusty thinks he killed her sister, based on that one comment. See if you can get him to talk about it some more. We're in this together, right?"

Hannah looked a bit tentative, then answered, "Why do you care about Juno? You don't even know him. And why haven't they arrested him yet, if they think he's the murderer?"

"He doesn't seem like the type to murder someone, Hannah, and I don't think they've connected the dots yet. They're looking for whoever made that call, and they neglected to talk to Dusty about it, or she would tell them. I suspect they have no idea he also called her, and she probably thinks they already know. But once they figure out it was him, well, he's not going to need a place to stay, that's for sure."

Hannah finally said, in a low voice, "OK, but I doubt if he'll talk about it—he hasn't so far. But I'll help you if you'll help me."

She continued, though now whispering. "My neighbor on the other side of the cafe told me he saw that ghost early this morning, and it was sitting on that big rock right behind the cafe. I'm worried sick. It's getting too close, hanging around the grounds here. And I'm having a real hard time sleeping at night ever since Callie was killed. I keep having nightmares. Please keep an eye out for me. I don't know if ghosts can harm people, but this is way too close for comfort."

"It's a deal," Bud said, "And don't worry, I'll figure out this ghost thing. Just give me some time."

He walked out the cafe door, not sure how he was going to figure out anything, yet alone something that he didn't even believe existed.

And Bud hadn't forgotten his gut feeling at Hays Creek Falls. He sure wasn't convinced that Juno Alaska was innocent, but he had to start somewhere.

# 18

"My jacket was right where I left it, hanging on a tree," Bud told Wilma Jean, draping it over a kitchen chair. "They hadn't even started cleaning the grounds yet. All the folding chairs were still out. They must be short-handed."

"You're a lucky man, Bud Shumway," said Wilma Jean, smiling. "In more ways than one. We've been invited to dinner in two weeks at the Redstone Castle with Dusty Jensen. It's a big to-do with only the finest dining, or at least that's what the invitation says, and I'm not sure if that means the food is the finest or the guests are. It's a special dinner in honor of her sister, Callie. It will include a wine tasting and music by the renowned Celtic harpist, Brannagh O'Brown."

"O'Brown?" Bud asked.

"She's half Irish," Wilma Jean said, handing Bud a hand-written invitation, obviously done by someone with a beautiful talent for calligraphy. Bud studied the invitation, which was lettered in silver and gold foil, then turned it over. "Sjoberg Design, Carbondale, Colorado," was embedded on the back in red foil.

"Very tasteful," Bud remarked. "I bet that cost a pretty penny. I wonder how many people she's invited. But I made a promise to myself at the memorial service, and it's one I intend to keep."

"What kind of promise?" Wilma Jean asked suspiciously.

"To never rent a suit again—actually, to never *wear* a suit again," Bud replied. "And I don't see how an invite like that is lucky."

"We'll get to see the inside of the castle."

Just then, Bud's phone rang.

"Yell-ow," Bud answered.

"Is this Bud Shumway?"

"It is."

"Bud, this is Dusty. I'm now living over at the castle, and I woke up this morning to find a complete stranger camped on the grounds. I sent Gene over to find out what was going on—you remember him from the memorial service, Callie's business manager—and he came back saying it was one of Callie's fans who had heard about the murder and is here to help."

"Well, that's awfully nice of him," Bud replied. "I guess there are some good things about being famous."

"No, you don't get it," Dusty sounded frustrated. "He has three dogs with him—two Basset hounds and a bloodhound. They're running all over the grounds sniffing everything. He told Gene he was going to hunt down the killer. Gene thinks he's loony and was afraid to run him off. We need to get him out of here."

Bud paused. "I guess you'll have to call the sheriff. I don't have the authority to tell anyone they can't be where they want to be, unless it's my own house or vehicle."

"Oh, for crying out loud," Dusty moaned. "Please, come over here and get rid of him. The sheriff says they're too busy and can't get here today, unless he's actually threatening us."

"Well, if he's nuts, I might be putting myself in some kind of danger," Bud dodged.

Dusty now sounded even more frustrated. "You used to be a sheriff. You know how to make people behave. Come out and I'll make it worth your time."

Last thing Bud wanted to do was get involved with a lunatic country-western fan. He'd seen a couple at Howie and the Ramblin' Road Ranger concerts, and they could get pretty out of hand, blowing air horns and shouting out the titles of tunes they wanted to hear and things like that.

Bud grinned at the thought, wondering if Howie was behaving himself and getting in more practice with the band. It suddenly occurred to him that maybe he could expedite Howie's career a bit if he were just a little more savvy.

"Say, Dust," Bud said congenially. "Thanks for the invite to the big party. We're supposed to R.S.V.P., so consider us as good as gold. We'll be there, but be forewarned, I won't be wearing a suit. And I'd like to ask you a favor."

She replied, her frustration now almost palpable. "I'll do anything if you'll come out and get rid of this lunatic. He's currently out in Callie's rose garden, doing who knows what. And the baying! I've never heard dogs that could make such a racket. Anything you want."

"Are you sure about that?" Bud asked.

"Just tell me, then get out here."

"OK. I have a friend who has a country-swing band. I think it would be really nice to play some of the kind of music Callie enjoyed at a dinner in her honor. And people could dance to it, too. I know you already have the harpist playing, but maybe they could play at the end or something."

"Brannagh O'Brown just cancelled on me. She got a gig playing for Bubba up in Aspen."

"Who's Bubba?"

"Oh, that's what ex-President Clinton's friends all call him. So, what does your friend charge?"

Bud hesitated, then shot for the moon.

"$1,500 a gig. That's only $500 each, a real bargain."

"OK, that's cheap enough. Tell them to come and they can play after dinner. Now will you get out here?"

"Problem is, Dust, they need prepayment for their gigs—you know how people cancel things."

Bud neglected to add that Howie's band had actually never had a paying gig, but he knew they would probably ask for prepayment if they ever did—maybe, anyway.

Dusty sounded relieved.

"OK, I'll have Gene give you a check when you get here. You're coming right away? Oh jeez, now he's at the front door."

"I'll be right there," Bud replied, grinning. "Make it out to Howard McPherson. Thanks, Dust, they'll be very pleased. I'm sure they were fans of Callie. Oh, and..."

Dusty replied, "What?"

"They'll need accommodations as part of the deal. You have 42 rooms out there, so I'll tell them they can stay at the castle. Will that work?"

"Alright," Dusty sighed. "But understand that Callie's wing is strictly off-limits. Now get out here."

"I'm on my way," Bud replied.

He hung up, smiling at Wilma Jean, who had been listening in and had a look of disbelief on her face.

For once, he couldn't wait to call Howie.

# 19

Bud had tried to call Howie while on his way to the Redstone Castle, but Howie hadn't answered, which Bud found worrisome. He figured he'd try again around dinner time. It was almost evening, and Howie would surely be home for dinner.

As Bud drove down the long narrow lane to the castle, he spotted a big white motorhome parked on the grass under the tall maple trees that edged the castle grounds. As he drove by, he noted that it had Indiana plates which bore the words, "Lincoln's Boyhood Home."

This had to belong to the guy with the hounds, Bud figured. It seemed pretty cheeky to Bud to actually just come down the lane, which was marked "Private, No Trespassing," and set up camp, just like that.

Bud then recalled coming down that same lane himself recently and then actually going up onto one of the castle decks and tossing off patio chairs.

He felt a bit sheepish, coming to run someone off for doing something similar to what he'd recently done. He wondered if the fellow felt the same way he had, like he just wanted to figure things out. Of course, now Juno the groundskeeper was gone and Dusty was there instead, probably making it a little tougher to just wander around.

As Bud drove down the lane, he thought back to the day he saw the tribute to Calico Callie on the Aspen TV channel. Hadn't the guy said there was a rumor that she'd been in a dispute with someone? Could that have been her sister, Dusty? Was it possible that Dusty had something to do with Callie's murder?

It seemed unlikely, and Bud wasn't usually much of one to pay attention to rumors, but in a murder case, the truth often surfaced in unlikely ways.

Bud could hear what sounded like a pack of hounds baying in the distance as he pulled up in front of the castle. He could also hear what sounded like someone shouting in the distance.

"Winston, Heidi, Sadie, you guys get back here *right now!*"

Bud figured it had to be the hounds guy. Since Hoppie was a Basset, Bud knew all about who a hound's true master was—their nose—and wondered if maybe the dogs weren't on the hunt. Sure enough, the baying seemed to be receding in the distance, like the dogs were running off. They seemed to be going up the valley in the direction of Hays Creek Falls.

Now a thin gray-haired fellow was running toward Bud. He came to Bud's car window and said, "Hey, would you mind following those dogs? No way I can do it in my big old clunker of a rig, not in time. If I don't catch them, I may not see them ever again. Mind if I hop in?"

Bud could now see Dusty looking out the window of the castle's foyer.

"Sure, jump in," he replied.

Dusty gave Bud a thumb's up as the man got into the pink Lincoln. She looked very pleased. Bud was surprised at how easy getting the intruder and his dogs off the castle grounds appeared to be.

"Name's Sprocket," the man offered. "Sprocket Obrochta. I used to race bicycles. Those dang hounds are nothing but a pain in the neck. Every time I lose one, I say I'm not getting another."

"Nice to meet you. I'm Bud Shumway. You lose them?" he asked.

"Oh, you know, not really lose them, but when they die, that kind of lose."

"Oh, sure," Bud replied. "I understand. I have a Basset myself."

Sprocket looked surprised. "You have a Basset? I don't meet fellow Basset lovers very often."

Bud had now turned the car onto the highway and was headed up the valley. He had his window open and could hear the sound of distant baying.

"Problem with doing this is that they're now on the other side of the river from us," Bud said to Sprocket. "Even if we catch up, will they swim across? Actually, you may not want them to. It can be deep and swift, even at this time of year."

Sprocket looked concerned. "That could be a problem."

"What are they chasing?" Bud asked.

"They saw a deer and took off," Sprocket answered. "I was walking them around the grounds, looking for a scent."

"A scent?"

"Yeah. I have an autographed photo of Calico Callie. I let them sniff it, then we went walking around to see if we could find her scent on the grounds."

"I bet her scent is all over the grounds."

"Oh, I know," Sprocket replied. "But I was hoping they'd find something unusual. You know that dark blue BMW sitting there? They went straight for that. I figure that must've been her car."

"That's her business manager's car. Maybe she rode in it at some time."

"They're good trackers," Sprocket said. "I've had them in lots of classes, right alongside professional police-dog trackers. I even volunteered them for search and rescue there back home, though nobody ever needed rescued. Nobody in Indiana ever does anything much outdoors, except during hunting season. Too hot and buggy or else too cold. If they said her scent was in that BMW, it had to be."

Bud could now see three little dark spots across the river in a large meadow. The dogs appeared to have stopped, though he knew hounds never rested when on the scent. They would literally run until exhausted. Something appeared to have the hounds confused.

Bud pulled over on the edge of the highway. Sprocket got out and yelled at the dogs, but it appeared they couldn't hear him over the sound of the river, as they just sat there.

"Is there some way I can get over there?" he asked Bud. "I need to get them before they take off again. Look at all that rugged country. They'll get lost for sure."

Sprocket nodded his head at the thick timber lining the red cliffs. There were several breaks where the dogs could easily climb from the valley into the forest above, yet not be able to get back down unless they remembered their route up.

Sprocket added, "Man, nothing like this where I'm from."

Bud had no idea how Sprocket could get across the Crystal River. Even at this time of year it had plenty of deep holes and a strong current that could easily sweep one off their feet, not to mention the many rocks one would have to negotiate. It seemed impossible to Bud.

And now the dogs were gone again, continuing up the valley. Sprocket jumped back into the car and they took off again, but Bud was beginning to think they were on an impossible quest.

## 20

"You do realize you're trespassing by camping there on the castle grounds and running around all over the place," Bud said to Sprocket as they drove on.

"Trespassing? Isn't it a public place?"

"No, of course not. It's Callie's private home, or was, anyway."

"So, I'm trespassing?"

It seemed to Bud that Sprocket was having a hard time with the concept.

"Doesn't Indiana have places with private grounds like that?"

Sprocket looked incredulous. "Sure, of course they do. But I for some reason thought, since it was a castle, it was like a big museum or something. I wasn't aware Callie actually lived there. So, I'm trespassing? Will I get arrested?"

"You would've already been arrested if the sheriff's office wasn't an hour away and his deputies overworked. Callie's sister is there now, and she actually did call the sheriff."

Sprocket looked shocked. "I've never trespassed in my life, well not that I know of. Do you think she'll have my RV towed?"

"No, she called me to come and talk to you. She told me they'd talked to you, and you refused to leave."

"No, this guy just came over and asked what I was doing, but he never told me it was private property. We talked a bit about Calico Callie, then he left. I told him the truth—I'm here to try to help solve her murder. It hit me in a big way, as I've been a fan of hers for years. I'm retired and have plenty of time on my hands."

Sprocket looked thoughtful. "The guy acted like he thought I was nuts. I'm country, and you could tell he's city, and never the twain shall meet. But did you know Callie? Are you part of the family or something?"

"I know her sister, Dusty, but only in a cursory way. Never met Callie. Dusty called me because I used to be a sheriff."

The highway now made a big sweeping curve, and Bud could see a lane take off to the left, where a small wooden bridge crossed the river. He turned off the highway and drove down the lane to a small log house with a fenced-in lawn that was lined with old mining apparatus, things like old ore cars, rusted metal wheels, and various piles of what looked to be some kind of ore—big quartzite rocks with silver streaks and shades of green and purple.

There, an older man in a straw cowboy hat stood looking at three hound dogs in his yard. He had set out a bowl of water, but the dogs were too busy panting to drink, though every once in a while one would stick his long nose in and slobber all over.

Typical crazy hound dogs, Bud thought, wondering how the old guy had managed to catch all three.

"These your dogs?" the guy asked as Bud and Sprocket got out.

Sprocket ran over, hugging one of the hounds. "I was worried sick about you idiots."

He turned to the guy. "How in the world did you catch them? When they're on the hunt, they won't come for anything."

The old guy grinned. "I could hear them coming for a long ways, and I used to have a bluetick coonhound, so I know a little about how their puny little brains work. I opened the gate and they came right in. It helped that the deer came right through here ahead of them— deer come through here all the time to get down to the river."

Sprocket was now looking around. "Nice place! I'm Sprocket

Obrochta, and this is Heidi, Sadie, and Winston. Thanks for catching them. I was worried I'd never see them again. Man, you must be an ex-miner or something with all this junk."

"Gus Dearhammer," the man answered. "Pleased to meet you."

He shook hands with Sprocket and Bud both, then said, "I used to have a mining claim, but I just sold it."

Bud thought about how Juno had said Callie had grubstaked Gus. Had she known he'd sold the mine? Or had he sold it after her death? Had he intended to pay her back for grubstaking him?

Bud asked, "Where was it?"

"Up in Lead King Basin," Gus replied. "Lead King Number 2. Worked it for 23 years. Broke my back and can't do much now. Crushed a vertebra and been stoved up ever since."

Gus was Callie's nearest neighbor, even though it was a half-mile or so to the castle.

"Say," Sprocket said thoughtfully to Gus. "I'm camped over at that big manor house down the road, and I need a new camp spot. Would you be interested in renting out a space here? Back there under the trees would be nice—right by the river."

Bud was surprised at Sprocket's forwardness, then figured he must be of the "ask and ye shall receive" camp.

"For how long?" Gus asked.

"I don't know. Until Calico Callie's murder is solved," Sprocket replied.

"You a lawman?" Gus asked, surprised.

"No, but I served for 35 years in the Indiana Criminal Investigation Division. Raced bicycles on the weekends." Sprocket said.

Bud was surprised, but said nothing.

"Well," Gus answered. "I suppose you can camp here for a bit, but be forewarned that I've been having problems with a bear coming around. Keep a clean camp. No outdoors cooking and no trash, or I'll have to run you off."

He then added, "And if you see anyone snooping around, feel free to shoot 'em. Don't shoot the bear, but if you see a guy named Juno Alaska, shoot away all you want. You can consider that your rent."

# 21

Bud was sitting on the front steps of the cottage, holding the phone away from his ear, trying to make sense of what Howie was saying.

It was dawn, and he'd been watching the first hints of sunrise light up high wispy clouds that looked to be mares' tails, high cirrus clouds that are precursors to storms. As the sun rose over the canyon rim, it lit up one particular stand of red aspen, making it glow a brilliant scarlet color. He'd been getting ready to take a few photos when his phone had rung.

Howie was excited. "I found it, Sheriff! Do you think Old Man Green had anything to do with it? I can't believe it, but you never know what lurks in the heart of man or however that goes. It was right there behind his barn."

"What was it exactly that you found, Howie?" Bud asked, wishing he had a cup of coffee to clear his mind.

"The Land Cruiser, Sheriff!"

Howie was talking so fast that Bud could hardly keep up.

"I was out driving around in Maureen's VW Bug—I haven't asked the mayor yet about your FJ because I kind of hate for him to know about the Land Cruiser being stolen—and I decided to cruise on down by Old Man Green's farm, and I thought I saw something there behind his barn, and I stopped and pulled over but he wasn't home, so I walked back behind his barn and there it was! Just sitting there."

"Was the key in the Hide a Key holder?"

"It was. So whoever stole it, they were at least considerate enough to put the key back. I need to fingerprint everything and see what we can find."

"Well," Bud replied, "That's good news, Howie. Was anything damaged?"

"Nope. Everything was just like before. It wasn't even dirty, and they even left some gas in the tank. They probably took it to the car wash before they left it at the farm. Probably trying to hide their tracks. You know how that goes, they wash off the dirt so you can't figure out where they've been with it. I just hope they didn't commit any crimes with it."

"Well, it doesn't seem very likely that someone would steal a sheriff's vehicle in Green River, go rob a bank or something with it, then return it to the area where they stole it. It kind of stands out with its light bar and 'Emery County Sheriff' sign on the doors," Bud replied.

Howie now paused, then said, "You know, Bud, it would make a perfect get-away vehicle. I never even thought of that. Nobody would think the robber would be in a sheriff's car. Maybe whoever stole it is part of some big ring of crooks—smart crooks. I hope I don't get implicated in something."

"I wouldn't worry too much, Howie. Probably just some kids out joy riding. They'll tell their grandkids someday about how they once stole a sheriff's car back when they were wild and crazy. But you might want to put that key someplace a little harder to find than under the front bumper."

Howie replied, "Oh, I know, Sheriff. I already moved it to under the back bumper. Anyway, what are you doing up so early?"

"Just out taking a few sunrise photos, Howie. And I could ask you the same question."

Howie said, "Well, I was hoping I wouldn't wake you up. I know you usually get up early. I couldn't sleep, I was so excited, so I decided to just get up."

"Well, it is exciting to get the Land Cruiser back, that's for sure," Bud said.

"Yeah, that's good, but I'm excited about something else, too."

Bud waited for Howie to continue, leaning back, thinking of the conversation he'd had with Wilma Jean the previous evening down by the river, where she'd told him about this thing called the 'Slow Movement.'

According to his wife, its basic philosophy was that everything should be done at the right speed, and that faster wasn't always better. He wondered if maybe Howie hadn't joined their ranks.

Finally, Howie continued, "Sorry, Sheriff, but I had to think about why I'm so excited, other than finding the Land Cruiser, that is. But Bud, I *am* really excited, that's for sure."

He paused, and Bud was ready to start the countdown when Howie added, "I guess it's because Maureen told me we finally have our first paying gig. I'm having a hard time wanting to go to work. I want to go practice, instead."

Bud knew that Wilma Jean had called Maureen the previous day to report the news about playing at the castle after Bud hadn't been able to get ahold of Howie.

"Well, don't let it stress you out, Howie. There probably won't be that many people there."

"I'm trying not to, but I can't help it. And I knew all along you'd be the right guy to be our business manager. I can't believe it—$500 each? That's crazy."

Bud groaned. He had no desire to be Howie's business manager. He reached for the beads in his pocket, but his pants were a bit twisted from getting dressed when he was half asleep, and he couldn't get to them.

"Anyway, Sheriff, I gotta go. I need to get out of here before Maureen wakes up," Howie said.

"Why's that?"

"She's mad at me again. I don't feel like getting yelled at. I'll buy her some more flowers this afternoon, and by then she should be over it."

"Anything in particular?" Bud asked.

"I got in late again last night. She wouldn't even let me explain."

"Why were you late?"

"Well, see, I found the Land Cruiser, so I drove it back to the office. That meant Maureen's VW was still out at Old Man Green's. He wasn't around to help me out, so I had to walk back to get Maureen's car."

"That's a good five-mile walk," Bud noted.

"Yeah, and I'm sore again today, though not as bad as the last time. But I have to admit I was kind of paranoid out there walking along in the dark all by myself."

"In Green River?"

"Yeah, I was thinking about whoever stole the Land Cruiser. Made me worry a bit. I was hoping Maureen's bug would still be there when I got back out to the farm."

"And it was, wasn't it?"

"Yep, right where I left it. But say, you having any luck with that case over there?"

"Not really, Howie. I haven't had anything much to go on. I guess it's not the end of the world if the time comes for us to leave for Radium and it's not solved, though I'd sure like to know who did it."

"Well, good luck. We'll be over there soon, and maybe I can help you out."

"Thanks, Howie. I appreciate that," Bud replied.

As they said goodbye, Bud noted the light on the trees was now gone, the brilliant scarlet color now faded to a dull red. The sun was now beginning to light up the valley with a harsher more direct light.

The "magic hour," as photographers call it, was over, that time when the sun is near the horizon and its light is more reddish due to the greater depth of atmosphere.

Bud stood to go back inside when he noticed a shadow moving over at the Ice House Cafe. At first, he thought it might be the bear again, but he then knew it couldn't be when it opened the front door and went inside.

Bud looked at his cell phone. It was 6:30 a.m. He was pretty sure the cafe opened at seven. It had to be Hannah, but why was she coming home at this hour?

The upstairs lights went on, and soon, the figure was opening the window that looked out toward the cottage. Bud could now see that it was indeed Hannah.

She now leaned out and looked directly at Bud, then started yelling out, "There's blood everywhere, Mr. Shumway. Blood on the forehead. Blood on the headboard. Blood on the moon and blood on the Unknown's Tomb. The zombie will pay, she'll pay with her life."

Bud slowly turned and went inside, locking the door. He then carefully took his Ruger from its holster in the bedroom closet and loaded it, trying not to wake his wife.

# 22

Bud had made some coffee in the percolator pot and was now sitting again on the front steps of the cottage in the bright sunlight, drinking coffee and thinking about what Hannah had said, twirling the string of beads that he now wore around his neck, hidden under his shirt collar.

No more fiddling with trying to reach them in his pants pocket, and given what had just transpired, he knew he would have lots more fiddling to do before he could figure anything out.

The incident with Hannah had been very disturbing, but he now realized that part of the reason wasn't just *what* she'd said, but *how* she'd said it. She had sounded really strange, her voice like someone in a horror movie. She hadn't sounded at all like Hannah.

He decided to go on over to the cafe, which was now open, and talk to Hannah and see why she'd said what she did. It was the only way to figure things out, confront her directly, and he wasn't one to let things like this go. Her comment had been disturbing, and Bud wanted to know exactly what was going on.

Just then, he saw a white SUV coming down the street. It had a light bar on top, and as it got closer, he could see the insignia on the side: Gunnison County Sheriff.

Now the vehicle stopped right in front of the cottage, and a deputy leaned out the window and asked, "Do you bite?"

Bud was taken back and not sure what to say. It was turning out to be a very strange morning.

"No, I guess not, unless maybe you were to bite me first," he replied.

The deputy now got out and leaned against his SUV. "Well, my son Jeff says you bark, so I just wanted to make sure you didn't bite, too."

The deputy looked amused as he held out his hand.

"I'm deputy Chuck Schofield, and I sometimes cover Redstone for Sheriff Mason. I live in Marble. My son goes to the grade school down the street."

Bud shook hands, then said, "My dogs are bad influences. But where's Gunnison County? I thought we were in Pitkin County here."

Chuck replied, "It starts just up the road. The counties around here don't match up with the towns. Sheriff Mason told me about you being a private detective and working on the Calico Callie case. I'd like to talk with you a bit. He said you might know where Juno Alaska is—and no, don't tell me it's south of Anchorage."

Bud now leaned against the sheriff's SUV, next to Chuck.

"I'm not sure where Juno is," Bud replied. "I barely know the guy. Are you looking to arrest him?"

"Yes, exactly. Mason has evidence that Juno's the one who called 911. I guess he said something that was self-incriminating. Two deputies came down here last night to the castle, but he was gone. He's been fired and nobody has any idea where he went. The sheriff thought you might know."

Bud was surprised that Sheriff Mason gave him credit for knowing anything.

"I really don't know," Bud replied. "But I did hear a rumor that he was going up to the Lead King Mine to work, but I don't know how accurate it is."

"Who told you that?" Joe asked.

"I can't tell you. If I do and they find out, they won't talk to me again, and I think they may know more about all this than I do."

Bud felt somewhat like he was betraying Hannah's confidence, but then again, he had no right to hinder justice—or possible justice, anyway.

"Lead King Basin's a real bear to get in and out of," replied Chuck. "Four-wheel all the way, and at one place, you drive across a big scree field that feels like it's moving under you. I'll need help if I do find him."

Bud groaned. "I'm not a lawman."

"Didn't you used to be?" asked Chuck.

"Yeah, but I didn't enjoy putting my life in danger even when I was getting paid." Bud replied. "Last thing I want to do is go help arrest someone, especially when I'm not so sure the man should be arrested."

Chuck replied, "Sheriff Mason has probable cause or he wouldn't have issued an arrest warrant."

"I'm not sure a 911 message when one's half drunk is probable cause," Bud replied, then sighed. He knew Mason's office was overworked. Maybe if he gave Chuck a hand it would make things less likely to go south if Chuck did find Juno.

He sighed. "All right, I'll go along for the ride. But I first need to go over to the Ice House Cafe and get a bite to take along. Haven't even had breakfast yet."

"I need to go get gas," Chuck replied. "And thanks. I appreciate the help. I'll be right back."

As Chuck drove away, Wilma Jean came outside. She put her hand on Bud's arm and said, "Hon, we need to leave—today"

Bud was surprised. "Leave? I thought we'd decided to stay. What's going on?"

"I was up when Hannah yelled all that weird stuff out the window. I'm that 'zombie' she threatened. I have no idea what's going on, but I have a bad feeling about it, and the tone of her voice makes me wonder if she wasn't involved in all this somehow. This is turning out to be the opposite of a vacation. Everywhere I go, people stare at me like I'm someone dead."

"Well, I don't blame you one bit," Bud replied, putting his arm around her shoulders. "But I just can't picture Hannah involved in anything like that. Like you told me earlier, she's way too nice."

"What did that deputy want?" Wilma Jean asked.

"He's looking for Juno."

"We're going home today, Bud," she said, then went back inside.

Bud knew what the unsaid part of her statement was: "Don't make promises you can't keep."

He turned and walked across the grassy lawn that separated the cottage from the cafe. He knew Wilma Jean was probably already packing their stuff.

He opened the door to the Ice House Cafe. He wanted to talk to Hannah, get something to eat, then talk to Wilma Jean and see if she would postpone the trip home just one more day, though he was pretty sure he knew what the answer would be.

## 23

Hannah stood by a booth where a family of four sat, two young girls with who Bud assumed were their parents. She seemed to be enjoying her role of historian, telling them all about the Ice House Cafe as they listened attentively.

"See, ice houses were needed back then because there wasn't any refrigeration," Hannah nodded at one of the young girls, who looked to be about eight and had hair so black it was almost blue. "This was the perfect spot for an ice house since it was right by the river, and back then, the river would freeze solid, or pretty close, so it was a good source of ice."

"Did they find fish in the ice later?" asked the young girl.

"Gee, I don't know," Hannah answered. "I never thought of that. But they would cut these big blocks of ice from the river and store them inside here, packed with sawdust for insulation, then use it during the warmer months to keep their food cool. How would you like a cold drink with a chunk of river ice floating in it?"

"Right now?" asked the other girl, who looked a bit older. "I think I'd rather have regular ice, please, since it won't have bugs and twigs in it."

Hannah laughed, gave them their check, then walked over to where Bud was sitting in the back booth.

"Morning, Bud," she greeted him amiably. Bud noted that she seemed to have no vestiges of the anger she'd displayed earlier while yelling out the window.

"Hi, Hannah," he replied. "How are you feeling this morning?"

"Oh, I'm fine," she replied. "You having your usual coffee and ice cream?"

"No, I'd like to order three box lunches instead. Can I get one tuna, one roast beef, and one vegetarian sandwich, each with chips and some kind of salad?"

He would get lunch for himself, Chuck, and Wilma Jean, though he knew she wouldn't want to go along, and he preferred she didn't, to be honest, as things could go south. He was pretty sure he could talk her into staying one more day if he could talk to Hannah and figure out what had been going on.

Hannah said, "I have some pasta salad I just made. Not bad, if I don't say so myself."

"That'll work," Bud replied. "Throw in three cold sodas, too."

"You guys going on a picnic? Deputy Chuck going with you?" she asked suspiciously, then added, "For somebody on vacation, you sure hang around with the working folks a lot—especially the ones from the academy."

Bud was again irritated, but tried not to show it. It seemed to him that Hannah had her pulse on everything he did lately.

"I doubt very much if Chuck attended a police academy," Bud replied. "He's going to show me Lead King Basin. I don't have any way to get up there otherwise, since it's four-wheel drive."

Now Hannah looked disturbed. She leaned over and said quietly, so no one else could hear, "You know that's where Juno went. Is the law looking for Juno?"

"Yes," he replied. "But you didn't hear it from me."

Bud suddenly felt like he was playing both sides of the equation, and he wasn't so sure he liked the feeling. He didn't want to lie to anyone, and yet, his gut told him Juno wasn't guilty. He'd been around enough guilty people, and Juno just didn't have that same feel. It was an intangible thing, something he could never describe, and he just didn't think Juno had it in him to murder someone he worked for and admired, or had said he did, anyway.

"By the way, Hannah," Bud asked, "What did you mean by what you said this morning?"

"What do you mean, what I said? You mean about the ice? I guess it could have had fish in it. I'd never given it any thought before."

"No, earlier, when you were yelling out the window."

"Yelling out the window?"

"Hannah, early this morning, around 6 a.m., you opened your window and yelled out some stuff at me. You know what I'm talking about. I'm just asking you to explain it more."

Bud thought that Hannah looked truly mystified, yet surely she had to remember it. You don't get worked up enough to yell at someone about blood and zombies and then forget it in a few hours.

"I think you have me confused with someone else. I didn't even wake up until late. For some reason my alarm didn't go off, and I was worried about not opening the cafe on time. Even if I had wanted to say something to you, I wouldn't have had time. And about blood? I want nothing to do with blood, except my own. You must've been dreaming."

She turned and went into the kitchen, leaving Bud feeling confused. How could she not recall the incident? She had to be lying, yet she seemed sincere. Was someone else staying with her?

Bud sat, fiddling with the beads around his neck, when Hannah finally returned, three sack lunches in hand, and handed him the bill.

"You have someone staying up there with you?" Bud asked, then quickly added, "Look, I'm not trying to be nosy, but someone was yelling at me this morning from your window."

"This is a small town," Hannah replied, taking the money Bud gave her. "A very small town. You need any change back?"

"No, keep the change."

"Word gets out pretty darn fast if someone's loony," Hannah

added, sticking the money in her apron pocket. "I won't tell anyone, but you should be careful what you see around here."

"I can't help what I see," Bud replied with irritation.

"You maybe can't help what you see, but you *can* help what you tell others you see. If you saw someone yelling at you from my window, you can be sure you weren't seeing reality. Maybe you should quit running around so much and get some sleep."

She turned to go, then turned back and added, "I don't think you're going up to Lead King to see the scenery. If you find Juno, tell him I can't go his bail. I knew it would be just a matter of time before he got himself arrested. I don't know if he did it or not, but he's a good place for you guys to start."

"I thought you said he couldn't have done it," Bud replied.

"That was before Gus came by the cafe yesterday evening. He told me Juno's been over by his place out in the meadow secretly burying stuff," Hannah replied. "And I guess he's even been over at Gus's house in the night snooping around. Gus is pretty worked up over it."

"Burying what kind of stuff?" Bud asked.

"Gus couldn't find anything, but he knows he's hiding something. Anyway, you guys have a nice picnic up in the basin—just don't get stuck, 'cause Chuck's the only deputy around here, and he sure wouldn't be able to rescue you if you're stuck in his vehicle."

With that, Hannah walked back into the kitchen, leaving Bud just as mystified as when he had first walked in the door.

## 24

Bud had talked Wilma Jean into staying a few more days, empha-
sizing how much Chuck needed his help. She had at first been reluc-
tant, but their friends Doc Richardson and Millie had called and told
them they'd decided to come on up to Redstone from Palisade the
next afternoon, and neither Wilma Jean nor Bud wanted to miss
seeing them, so it had all worked out.

Bud grabbed his camera, a jacket, and the sack lunches and sodas,
then started to jump into the patrol vehicle with Chuck, but had
instead gone back inside and got his Ruger and shoulder holster.

As he and Chuck started down the Redstone Boulevard, he could
see Hannah watching from the window of the Ice House Cafe.

For some reason, Bud had a strange feeling that not all was as it
seemed with Hannah, but he couldn't put his finger on what it might
be, other than her strange words to him early that morning. It had
almost seemed like she was threatening Wilma Jean, and the whole
thing had an ominous feel to it.

Maybe his wife was right, Bud mused, and they should leave. She
did seem to have some intuition when it came to knowing what to do.
He'd often thought she would make a much better detective than he
would, as she'd often given him astute insights into solving crimes

when he'd been sheriff. But having Doc and Millie here should ease things, Bud figured, though he had no idea how long they would stay.

Bud wasn't sure whether to be glad or disappointed about the trip into Lead King. On one hand, he was looking forward to seeing the basin, one of Colorado's historic mining districts, and having a local give him the tour would be a good way to do it, especially when the fall colors were peaking. But on the other hand, he was dreading running into Juno and was secretly hoping Juno was elsewhere.

They had just reached the Redstone Inn and were turning onto Highway 133 when Bud's phone rang.

"Yell-ow," he answered.

"Hon," Wilma Jean replied, "I just watched the news, and there's some weather coming in—an early fall storm."

Bud thought of the mares' tails he'd photographed earlier.

"When's it supposed to get here?" he asked, noting the sky was still a bluebird blue.

"Late this evening. It's a really fast-moving storm coming in from the northwest bringing snow and unseasonably cold air. They're predicting heavy snow above 9,000 feet. I looked it up on the Internet, and the Lead King road crests at 10,800 feet. You're going to be surrounded by 14,000 foot peaks. I think you guys might consider turning around."

Bud replied, "We'll be back long before anything hits, hon, not to worry. But thanks, we'll keep an eye out."

As Bud hung up, Chuck remarked, "I checked the weather this morning. I think we have lots of time to get up there and back. We'll come back early if need be."

As they drove up the valley, Bud thought that some of the peaks reminded him of Glacier National Park, where he and Wilma Jean had gone on their honeymoon some years ago. As they drove further on and the mountains loomed even higher, he was enjoying the scenery, but noted that he just didn't have the enthusiasm for these beautiful mountains as he did the for desert back home, what he called the Big Empty.

He tried to analyze it, figure it out, as it made no sense to him to feel this way. There was no contest that the mountains were stunning scenery, easily more scenic than the scrub desert around Green River. One could stop every hundred feet or so along the highway and take photos that could be on the cover of any calendar, they were that scenic.

Back home, the Big Empty stretched as far as one could see, terminating in the distant flanks of the Henry Mountains to the south, the San Rafael Reef and Swell to the west, and Pinion Mesa way over in Colorado to the east. To the northeast, the Bookcliffs stood above the town itself, their abrupt flanks unclimbable by all but levitating desert bighorn sheep. The desert views were long and sweeping, but those here in the mountains often were, also.

The Green River Desert was typically the monotone yellow-brown that characterized the Mancos Shale Formation, an ancient sea bed, where Bud had often found sharks' teeth and marine fossils.

Here, Colorado's West Elk Mountains towered over everything in shades of distant blues and greens, with the high mountain tops already bearing a coat of white from early autumn snows. And even better, the vast flanks of these mountains were now like magic carpets of red and gold where the aspens showed off their fall colors.

There was nothing like the crisp cool air here, and Bud loved it—but nights in the mountain valleys were nothing like the balmy nights in the desert, where one could sleep with no need for a blanket, lying under the starry night sky like the nomadic Native Americans must have. Here in the mountains, one had to keep the windows closed at night or risk waking up with what Wilma Jean called popsicle toes.

The mountains were a photographer's paradise, especially this time of year, so why wasn't he happier to be here? He was actually counting the days until this so-called vacation would end and he and Wilma Jean would go back to the desert.

He turned to Chuck and asked, "You from here originally?"

"Fourth generation," Chuck replied. "I don't know if you've ever heard of Schofield Pass, but it was named after my great-great-grand-father, Judge B. F. Schofield, who founded the town of Schofield. The pass connects Marble to Crested Butte and tops out at 10,722 feet.

Fourteen people have died up there to date, all in rigs that slid off the road near the Devil's Punchbowl. It's supposedly the most dangerous pass in Colorado. Only a few inches wider than a pickup, cambers outwards, is rocky, and drops straight into the river."

Bud said, "Sounds pretty hairy. You grew up here? All your life?"

"Yeah," Chuck replied, "Except a couple of years at the police academy over on the Front Range in Denver. Hated the city, and when I came back I swore I'd never leave."

Bud remembered what Hannah had said about Bud hanging with people from the academy—it appeared she was right after all.

Bud asked, "Do you ever get claustrophobic with all these mountains towering over you?"

"Claustrophobic? No, never even occurred to me," answered Chuck.

"I guess it's what you grow up with, that's where you're most comfortable," Bud replied thoughtfully. "See, I can see and appreciate the beauty here and realize there's nothing like it, but yet my comfort zone is back in the dry and desolate desert."

"Dry and desolate—yup, that's what desert means, isn't it?" Chuck asked, grinning at Bud. "But I understand what you're saying. My wife and I spent two weeks in Hawaii last year and I couldn't get over how beautiful it was, but I was happy to get back to my mountains."

"Well, I guess I'm just a desert rat at heart," Bud said.

"And I'm a mountain marmot at heart," Chuck replied, laughing.

"And what's interesting is we're the same species," Bud commented. He paused, then asked, "But do you really think Juno killed Calico Callie? I don't know how much you know about the case."

"I find it hard to believe," Chuck replied as they passed a sign that said, "Marble Town Limit, Elevation 7,950."

He continued, "I didn't know him very well, but I'd see him around town once in awhile. He seemed pretty mild mannered. But I've had people do things you would never expect, like the time mousy little Bernie Stevens whacked her husband, Rob, on the head with an iron skillet for eating all the Rocky Road ice cream. Rob called me, then declined to press charges—forgave her since she was pregnant."

Bud laughed. "I've had a few of those myself. Like the time I stopped a local farmer's wife and asked to see her license. She handed me her husband's. When I told her I needed to see hers, she said she'd been driving just fine for 40 years on his."

Chuck grinned. "Man, we should get together and write a book. Problem is, nobody would believe it. Well, here we are in Marble. I'm gonna swing by my place and get the Jeep."

He pulled up by a small log cabin that had an open-top black Jeep Wrangler in the drive.

Chuck added, "This is Blackie. We call him the Black Jeep of the Family. I was going to call him Moose because sometimes he goes crashing through the woods but is usually more in control than he lets on, just like a big moose."

"Why switch over? Isn't what we're in four-wheel drive?" Bud asked.

"It is, but it's too long for where we're going—lots of tight switchbacks, not to mention the gear ratios are too high. Blackie's been modified to crawl up and down these steep grades like a mountain goat. He's got a beefed-up suspension and extra lift, plus heavier skid plates."

Bud grabbed his stuff and got into the Jeep, the high mountains that towered over him making him feel a bit intimidated.

He knew he was about to get even more out of his element, but he also knew he would make the most of it. He was excited to see if he could get some good photos, something to show Howie back home and maybe even enter in the next photo contest up at the museum in Price, if he managed to live through it all.

## 25

Chuck slowly drove down the dirt streets of the tiny town of Marble, stopping at an intersection to let an ice-cream truck go through.

As they waited, Bud swore he knew the song the truck was playing, but he couldn't quite place it.

"What's that song?" he asked.

"It's the theme from the Godfather," replied Chuck.

"Of course," Bud grinned. "Perfect for an ice-cream truck, eh? Are there even enough kids here to support one?"

Chuck replied, "No, Marble has only about 130 people. That's Barb Somerset. She's a real character, converted the truck into an RV and lives in it. She always plays music when she drives around town. She came here from Kansas City, left everything behind, including a career as a physician's assistant, and now lives in that truck year-round."

"Must be cold in the winter," Bud remarked.

"No, because she goes to Arizona," answered Chuck.

They were soon on the edge of the little town with its rustic houses, their yards lined with chunks of marble.

"Where exactly is the marble quarry?" Bud asked. "We saw some big chunks along the Crystal River on our way to Redstone. Guess they must've fallen off the old railroad."

Chuck replied, "The Yule Quarry's across the valley about four miles, up on the side of the mountain. Those chunks you saw were used to stabilize the railroad grade."

"Marble for rip-rap?" Bud asked. "Seems like kind of an expensive way to go."

"It is," Chuck answered. "But back then, they had to use what they had, and you'll notice they were smaller chunks, worth less. But Yule marble is the finest marble in the world. You'll see it in lots of buildings, including the Lincoln Memorial and the Tomb of the Unknown Soldier. It's metamorphosed limestone and has a really fine grain that makes it almost glow in the sun."

They had now left town and were on a smooth dirt road, following the edge of a turquoise-blue lake that had a few fishermen on its shores.

Chuck continued, "This is Beaver Lake. We're going to be crawling up Daniel's Hill in about a mile—it's a 600-foot climb. And that's just the start."

Bud groaned to himself, then said, "Hows about we just stop here and try out the fishing?"

Chuck grinned. "We probably should. Anyone with any sense has left Lead King Basin for the season.'

Bud added, "It was just a rumor I heard about Juno being there, and I have no idea how valid it was."

Chuck added, "And there's a big storm coming in—all good reasons to turn around. But in all honesty, if you've never seen Lead King Basin, you're in for the trip of a lifetime."

"I've already had a few of those trips," Bud replied grimly. "And I only have one lifetime."

Chuck shifted into compound gear and they started up the steep grade of Daniel's Hill. After the steep climb, the road forked, and Chuck went to the right.

"This is actually a loop road, but we'll go this way and I'll show you the old Crystal Mill," Chuck said.

The road was narrow and rugged, and Bud held onto the Jeep's grab bar so he wouldn't bounce around as Chuck geared down, using the engine as a brake to slow them.

They soon passed the intensely green-colored Lizard Lake and dropped into Crystal Canyon, following the Crystal River as it trickled down a series of rocky cascades. At times, they were high above the river, the road no more than a narrow ledge.

"You should see this in the spring," Chuck commented, "Though you usually can't get in here until early summer because of huge snowbanks. But when you can, those waterfalls are so powerful they spray the road."

"That water's so clear you can see the rocks on the bottom," Bud mused, looking down tentatively from their perch high above. "Crystal clear."

Soon, they were across from a narrow old building with a high-pitched roof that sat perched on a rock ledge above a pool almost as green as Lizard Lake. The building's wood was so old that it had a deep brown patina that was almost black in places.

Chuck pulled over and they got out, Bud with camera in hand.

"This was a power mill built in 1892," Chuck said. "It generated power for mining operations. It's one of the most photographed sites in Colorado."

"What did they mine?" asked Bud. "Gold and silver?"

"Very little gold around here, but they did find lots of silver, lead, iron, copper and zinc. The Black Queen was silver, the Lead King was lead, copper, and silver, and the Copper King was, as you can guess, copper."

They poked around a bit, Bud taking lots of photos, some of a nice patch of blue columbine with the mill in the background. He noted the sun disappearing behind clouds.

"That storm's coming in pretty fast," Bud said to Chuck. "Are you sure it's wise to go on up into the high mountains?"

"We'll keep an eye on it," Chuck replied.

"You know, I think I may have figured out part of why I'm not a mountain man," Bud said.

"Why's that?"

"This country feels limiting to me. When I'm out in the desert, I can go just about anywhere I want, even if I have to walk. Sure, there are some big canyons down closer to Radium, but around Green River, the open country stretches for miles. You have a sense that you can explore without killing yourself on some steep slope or by falling off a cliff—or getting lost."

"Kind of a sense of freedom," Chuck added.

"Exactly. And I don't have to worry about running into a bear or mountain lion."

"Lots of people think of the desert as a hostile place, but maybe the mountains are actually more dangerous," Chuck said.

Bud replied, "As long as you have water, the desert's great."

"I'll have to get over your way sometime and see what you're talking about," Chuck said. "One thing about the mountains, you can't see what's coming in weather-wise. Let's decide what to do when we get up to the old mining town of Crystal. If we're lucky, the store will be open and we can get a candy bar. They also sell crystals and minerals."

Chuck then added, "On second thought, it's October. Nothing's open up here, and most everyone's gone. That place is a ghost town in the winter 'cause you can't get in there."

"We have these sack lunches from the Ice House," Bud replied. "I wouldn't mind stopping there and having a bite to eat. By the way, speaking of ghost towns, do you believe in ghosts?"

Chuck laughed, and they were soon in a large valley surrounded by towering peaks that looked down on fields of gold and red aspen, with a few cabins here and there, many crumbling into the ground, victims of decades of heavy snows.

Bud noted a few tendrils of gray clouds were now hanging over the highest peaks, portent of the incoming storm. A breeze had come up, blowing what remained of the summer daisies back and forth on their long stems.

They were soon in what was left of the old mining town of Crystal, home to a few hardy souls who appeared to have left for the winter. The general store was closed, and the town indeed looked like a good place for ghosts to hang around.

Just then, Bud caught a glimpse of an old red Toyota Celica driving down the town's only side street, heading in the opposite direction from them.

"Chuck, I don't think we're going to need to go any further, as much as I'd like to see the old Lead King Mine," he commented.

"Why's that?" asked Chuck.

"That was Juno Alaska."

Bud pointed at the old car as it disappeared around a corner, headed back toward Marble.

"And it appears he got word of the storm, because he's heading back to civilization. How he got that car in here is anybody's guess, and we'll see if he can get it back out."

## 26

"So much for having a nice quiet picnic in Crystal," Chuck said, turning the Jeep around to follow Juno. "Do you think he saw us?"

"I do," Bud answered. "But I don't think he's going to be able to outrun us in that Celica."

"A friend had one like that when I was in the academy," Chuck replied. "You'd be amazed at where they can go. I think he has about the same year they started making them front-wheel drive—1985, I think."

They could now see the Celica ahead, and Bud thought he saw Juno stick his head out the window and look back. Sure enough, the car sped up.

They were soon jostling over a stretch of rockslide rubble, and Bud thought they would surely catch up with Juno, but the little red hatchback kept bouncing along ahead of them and was actually starting to leave them behind.

They were now back along the creek, winding through a dense spruce forest peppered with aspens. They couldn't see ahead very far, and the red car seemed to have lost them.

Bud was amazed at how fast Juno was able to drive the car in four-wheel drive conditions, as they were having to slow down to a crawl in places to negotiate rockfall even in the Jeep.

Finally, they came around a bend to a section of loose shale and small boulders, and Bud could see the Celica once again. It appeared to have stopped next to a steep drop into the creek.

Chuck pulled up warily behind the car, and it was soon obvious that it was high-centered on a rock. Juno had fled the vehicle, and Bud knew he had to be nearby, as he hadn't had time to get very far, probably in the trees above them, as the bank into the creek was too sheer.

How had Juno known they were looking for him? Chuck's Jeep had no sheriff's insignia on it or anything else to indicate it belonged to a lawman.

"He knew we were after him, but how?" Bud asked.

Chuck replied, "Small town. Everyone in these parts knows everyone else, or at least who they are. We're talking a grand total of maybe 200 people total in Redstone and Marble, plus a few in the country in between. He knows this is my Jeep. And he knows we wouldn't be up here sightseeing this time of year with a storm coming in."

They got out and looked inside the car. It was dirty and the seat covers were torn. The floor on the passenger side was covered in old candy bar wrappers and plastic cups, as well as a few frayed newspapers. Bud picked one up and noted the headline announced Calico Callie's murder.

The breeze had now picked up into an outright wind, sudden gusts blowing aspen leaves from the trees, twirling them in clouds of red and gold.

"We need to get his car unstuck," Bud said thoughtfully. "He's not going to come out until we leave, and we don't want him to be stranded in here with this storm coming in. You have a jack and tow strap?"

They had soon jacked the car up, and Bud crawled underneath to try to dislodge the rock it was stuck on, but it was too big. He then wrapped Chuck's tow strap around the rock and guided it out as

Chuck pulled it with the Jeep. It was tricky, as they didn't want to damage the Celica, but they finally had the car unstuck and jacked back down.

Bud said, "I bet Juno's up in the timber, hidden, watching us right now, and as soon as we leave, he'll come back and drive out, though maybe wait an hour or two."

"I agree," Chuck replied. "He probably watched us get his car unstuck. We could go on down the road and set up a roadblock and wait for him."

"I think the important thing at this point is for him to get out of here before this storm hits," Bud replied with concern. "He doesn't appear to have any kind of cold-weather gear with him at all. If he does, he's wearing it, 'cause there's nothing here in the car."

Bud took his jacket from the Jeep and put it into the Celica, then added, "I'm leaving him our lunches, too. He may need them. We don't know if he's guilty or not, and we need a live suspect, not a dead one."

He put the lunches on the seat, then added, "I vote we just go home and leave him to his own devices. He'll either come out or he won't, but if we set up a roadblock, he'll see it and just bail and put himself in danger with this cold weather coming in."

"Good point," Chuck deferred. "I'd just as soon get home myself before this hits, and I still need to take you back to Redstone. Did you see any damage to his car while you were under there?"

"No, I think it's OK. If the predictions are correct, this road's gonna be under a few feet of snow before morning. I hope he decides to come on out."

Chuck paused, then said, "Well, if he doesn't, he'll be spending the winter here, dead or alive, and I'd put my money on the former, not the latter."

With that, they got back into the Jeep and started down the treacherous road to Marble, the wind now bending the aspens as the sky began to darken from the oncoming storm, making Bud glad he had a nice cozy cottage to go back to.

## 27

Bud woke with a start, wondering where he was. He'd been dreaming he was wandering around the marble quarry Chuck had told him about, and it was barely lit with a mysterious dull light.

The marble was luminescent, glowing in the dark, but not putting out enough light to really see where one was going. Everything had a sort of muffled feel to it, and it was cold—stone cold. He seemed to be lost, and was glad to awaken and realize it was a dream.

At first, he thought he was back at the bungalow in Green River and reached for the alarm clock on the nightstand to see what time it was. But he somehow knocked over a small lamp where the alarm should have been, the crash reminding him he was in the cottage in Redstone, not home.

He now sat up, wondering where Wilma Jean and the dogs were, then heard the comforting sound of her talking to them in the kitchen, where a percolator coffee pot was making its distinct bloop-bloop sound.

Bud pulled himself up and leaned back against the old Mission-style antique headboard. Everything in the cottage was antique—apparently even the pillows and mattress—and Bud had a stiff neck. He missed his down pillow and regretted leaving it back home.

He'd had that same pillow since he'd accidentally taken it with them when they'd stayed at Sheriff Hum and Peggy Sue's house in Radium, way back when. He'd offered to return it, but Peggy Sue had told him to keep it, that if he liked it well enough to steal it, he could have it.

She was, of course, kidding, but Bud had wondered if he maybe hadn't actually stolen the pillow, though at a subconscious level, as he liked the way he could puff it into different shapes and it would stay put.

Now, even though he'd figured out where he was, he couldn't figure out why it felt so different—then he suddenly realized it was snowing, diffusing the outside light and making it seem earlier than it was.

He almost felt as if he'd gone back in time with the old cottage's antiques and misty light, and for a moment he wondered what it must have been like to be a coal miner back in the town's heyday.

He knew it had to be a tough life, at least a lot tougher than his, even though the town of Redstone had running water and electricity, rare luxuries back at the turn of the 19th century. The benevolent John Osgood had wanted his miners to have better lives than most, though Bud suspected it was also a way of keeping a stable labor force.

Bud finally dragged himself from bed and looked out the window to the grassy lawn between the cottage and the Ice House Cafe. It appeared that a good three inches of snow had already fallen, with more still coming down. So much for the forecast calling for snow above 9,000 feet, Bud thought, as Redstone was only a mere 7,200 feet.

As he stood there, trying to wake up, he noticed something looked different over behind the cafe, but he couldn't quite put his finger on it. It looked like a giant icicle had fallen from the sky, landing point up, only a few feet behind the building. It was big, maybe a good 10-feet high and two-feet thick, and Bud was mystified as to where it could've come from.

He finally got dressed and stumbled into the kitchen, pouring himself a cup of coffee while Hoppie and Pierre totally ignored him, intently watching Wilma Jean, who was making something in a big bowl.

"Morning," she said. "I'm making dog biscuits. We ran out, and I don't want to drive the 15 miles to Carbondale, so I'm making my own."

"What's in it?" Bud asked.

"Mostly flour and butter," she replied. "And some bacon grease."

"Yum," Bud said, sipping his coffee. "Say, did you notice anything different over at the cafe?"

"You mean the giant icicle?" Wilma Jean asked. "They brought it in yesterday on a big truck, then used a hoist to set it in the ground. It's supposed to help advertise the cafe. You can see it from the highway."

"It looks like marble," Bud reflected.

"It is," said Wilma Jean. "I went over and watched and talked to Hannah. It was quite expensive. A local artist chiseled it from a block from the quarry."

She was now forming the dough into little biscuits shaped like bones and rabbits and even a few squirrels, though she was having trouble with the tails.

"I'm surprised Hannah can afford something like that," Bud said.

"She can't—a friend did it for her, on loan, an artist. Hannah told me she wants to sell the cafe and leave Redstone. She's had bad dreams ever since Calico Callie was murdered. I told her she wasn't the only one who wanted to leave, that we were leaving as soon as our company is gone. They'll be in late this afternoon, Bud, and I made reservations at the Redstone Inn for dinner at 5:30, so plan on it, hon. A little early so we can beat the crowd."

Wilma Jean gave each of the dogs a dollop of biscuit dough, then put the pan of biscuits into the oven.

Bud said, "I wonder if Dusty will be selling the castle soon. Surely it will be hers, once the estate is settled, as she's Callie's only relative."

Wilma Jean replied, "I would, if I were her. Who wants to live where their sister was murdered, or where they might also possibly get murdered, if the murderer isn't caught? Or maybe Dusty killed Callie so she could inherit all her money. Who knows?"

"Well," Bud replied. "I'm going to run over to Gus Dearhammer's. I need to talk to him about a few things."

"You have a 5:30 dinner appointment," Wilma Jean reminded him. "And Millie and Doc Richardson will be very disappointed if you're not here when they get in."

"I'll be right back."

Bud looked for his jacket for a moment, then remembered he'd left it in Juno's car. He wondered if Juno had gotten out in time or was now stuck in the snow up by Crystal.

He instead grabbed a sweater, then put on his holster with the Ruger and walked out the door.

He was barely aware of what he was doing, wondering where Hannah would go if she sold the cafe, if Dusty had killed Callie, and whether or not Callie's business manager, Gene Simpson, was somehow involved. He had no real reason to suspect either of the pair, but yet he did. It was important to cover all bases.

As he got into Wilma Jean's Lincoln, Bud thought again of Juno. He wondered if he still had what it takes to solve a crime, given that he'd been so off track, thinking Juno might be guilty when maybe he wasn't. But in his own defense, Bud thought, he hadn't really decided Juno was the killer, though a lot of evidence pointed that way.

He wondered what Juno had been burying out in the meadow near the castle. Maybe it was time to go take a look, in spite of the snow, and see what he could find, if anything. He needed something to judge if he were on the right or wrong course at this point.

Bud turned the big Lincoln toward the highway, slid a little on the icy bridge over the Crystal, then carefully pulled out and headed toward Gus's place. Snowflakes turned into large water droplets upon hitting his windshield, the sun struggling to break through heavy gray clouds.

## 28

Bud drove slowly down the highway, making first tracks, as the snow-plow hadn't yet reached his part of the world—or maybe they didn't plow the roads here until it got really bad, he thought, given that the area had such few people.

He caught a glimpse of the castle through the snowy trees. It looked like something from a fairy tale with its red stone walls contrasting with the pure white snow all around. It was quickly out of sight, hidden behind the timber.

Bud was soon at the turnoff to Gus's cabin, and he noted that Sprocket's RV was now parked down under the trees next to the river. It was an idyllic spot, or would be, Bud thought, if not for the four or five inches of snow covering everything. It looked to him that the big rig might have a bit of trouble getting out, given the incline it was parked on. Sprocket must like sleeping with his feet downhill, Bud mused.

Wanting to avoid getting stuck himself, Bud parked the big Lincoln where the drive had a bit of an incline going out, which would help him roll toward the highway if the drive got too slippery. But from the looks of things, the snow was now tapering off, and the clouds were quickly breaking, swirling around the higher ramparts of the red cliffs, the sun now nearly free.

He got out and walked through the gate into the grassy front yard, but soon noticed a set of boot tracks leading from the house to the far drive and on down to the RV. It appeared that Gus was down visiting Sprocket, so he would join them down there.

But once near the RV, he again noticed tracks, but now two sets of boot tracks and several sets of paw prints, and they all led out into the very meadow Bud himself was hoping to go check out.

He was suddenly suspicious. Why were they out in the meadow? Did Gus know where Juno had buried something, something that might provide evidence concerning Callie's murder? Or were they just out walking the hound dogs after the storm? And if they did find some kind of evidence, what would they do with it?

Should he turn around and leave or go out in the meadow and see what they were doing? He really didn't know either one of them very well, but they were supposedly all on the same page when it came to wanting to see Callie's murderer caught. And did Gus know something about Juno that would help solve the case? And why was he mad enough at Juno that he would tell Sprocket to shoot him?

Bud stood for a minute, the snow on the trees now starting to slowly melt and fall, making swooshing sounds at it hit the ground. A tree limb suddenly flipped upwards as the heavy snow that had held it down fell off, releasing it. Bud thought again of Juno, wondering if he'd made it out of Lead King in time.

He now walked out into the field that separated the castle grounds from Gus's place, tentatively following the tracks. He hadn't gone far when he met Gus and Sprocket and the hounds, all returning, the hounds on long leads, pulling Sprocket along.

Sprocket was carrying a clear plastic bag, and Bud could see it had blotches of mud on it. Whatever was inside was small and looked to be some kind of book.

Sprocket greeted Bud. He was obviously excited, holding the plastic bag up for Bud to see.

"I told you we'd find out who killed Callie," he said breathlessly as the dogs pulled him along.

"What did you find?" asked Bud.

"I think it's Callie's diary," Gus answered for Sprocket, who was being dragged onward by the hounds, eager to get back and get a drink or a treat or whatever it is hounds live for, other than their noses, Bud figured.

"Callie's diary?" Bud asked rhetorically. "You found her diary? Did you open it?"

"No, Sprocket doesn't want to get his fingerprints on it. But you can tell it's her diary," Gus added, "Because it says so right on the front. 'Journal of Callie Jensen.'"

"You guys have already compromised the fingerprints by picking it up," Bud said with concern. "If you give it to me, I'll get it to the sheriff's office, where it belongs. It might be a critical piece of evidence."

Sprocket had now stopped, the hounds panting, their heads down. He said, "We used the plastic bag to pick it up. But how do I know you're not going to take it and sell it or something? You're not a lawman, you're just like us. Why should I give it to you?"

Bud replied, "Well, one reason is because it might keep you boys from getting arrested for obstructing justice and hiding evidence in a murder case. That should be enough of a reason for any sane man."

"Don't get me involved in this," Gus said gruffly.

"I think it might be too late, since you were out there with Sprocket." Bud gave him a serious look.

He then turned back to Sprocket. "And if you're worried about me selling Callie's diary, I suggest we just wait here for a deputy to show up and take it straight from our hands. In fact, I'll call him right now."

He took his cell phone from his pocket.

Now Sprocket held his hand up. "Stop! Don't call just yet. Let's think this through a little. Look, if we all went in on this together and used our brains, we could help find the murderer and also keep the diary. I myself would pay a fortune for Calico Callie's diary, if I had a fortune to pay. She had a lot of loyal fans. We can make photocopies of all the pages and give that to the sheriff, then sell the diary."

Bud dialed Chuck's number, then said, "I thought you were all for catching Calico Callie's murderer. Isn't that why you came all the way out here from Indiana? The sheriff needs the original to fingerprint it. You should know that, having been with the Indiana Criminal Investigation Division for 35 years."

"I was an office flunkie," Sprocket said, now looking at the ground. "I did nothing but paperwork all day." He sounded disappointed.

"Hello, this is Deputy Schofield," a voice answered.

"Chuck, Bud Shumway here. Are you anywhere close to the Redstone Castle?"

"I'm in Redstone. Is that close enough?"

"You know where Gus Dearhammer lives?"

"I do."

"Can you come out here ASAP to collect some evidence in the Calico Callie case? It might turn out to be pretty important."

Chuck sounded surprised. "Evidence? At Gus's place?"

"Yeah, and Chuck, time is of the essence, as they say. See you soon."

Bud was worried Sprocket might change his mind.

"Roger. I'm on my way."

Bud hung up, studying Sprocket's face.

Finally, Sprocket said, "I'm sorry about all that. I really kind of got out of hand there for a minute. I don't know what came over me. I do want to see whoever murdered Callie brought to justice."

With that, he handed Bud the plastic bag that held Calico Callie's diary, then turned and dragged the panting dogs on down to his RV, taking them inside and shutting the door.

Gus looked at Bud and shrugged his shoulders, then said, "I was just along for the ride. But I know it was Juno who buried that there, and I know he was the one who murdered Callie."

Just then, Chuck drove up, and Gus quickly went inside, leaving Bud to wonder how he knew so much about Juno.

"I'm amazed at how quickly you got rid of that squatter," Dusty was telling Bud over a glass of spritzer. They were seated in two antique wrought-iron chairs on a small patio in the front of the castle.

She continued, "One minute he was here, the next, gone. You're very effective, I can say that."

Bud sipped his drink, trying to figure out the flavor. Peach? Raspberry? He wasn't sure if Dusty was still mad at him or not for refusing to work as her private detective, but the way she was kind of fawning over him, he suspected she had some new task she wanted him to do.

"Would you like to come inside?" Dusty asked, pointing to the front doors of the castle.

"I'm OK, but thanks," Bud replied. "My wife can't wait to take the tour, but we'll wait until the big party you're having. By the way, what flavor is this spritzer?"

"Watermelon," she answered. "I get it at a specialty shop in Aspen. It's imported from Greece. I had no idea Greece grew melons, did you? It's quite good, isn't it?"

"Delicious," Bud replied, though he really didn't think it was nearly as good as the watermelon spritzers Wilma Jean bought up in Price at Smith's Grocery. But he was now wondering if maybe he shouldn't be trying to develop a new market for Krider's melons. Someone who made spritzers might be interested in buying some.

Now Dusty took on a more serious air.

"I used to be married to a very wealthy man," she told Bud. "There was a time I would never have condescended to drink mere spritzers. We lived high on the hog, so to say, and drank only fine wines."

Bud replied, "Well, for me, spritzers are kind of a treat."

Dusty smiled. "I wasn't raised wealthy, though we always had enough. When Callie's estate finishes going through probate, I'll be considerably well-off, and once I sell this stupid castle, I'll be rid of this responsibility and can travel or do whatever I want. But how much do you want for getting rid of that nasty man with the dogs?"

Bud replied, "Dusty, all I did was say hello to him, then give him a ride a couple of miles. He's still in the neighborhood—staying over on Gus Dearhammer's property, your neighbor. He's actually an OK guy."

Bud decided not to mention that Sprocket had found Callie's diary, and probably on the castle grounds.

He continued, "But the deal was that you have my friends play at the party, remember? No need to pay me, but I do need to get a check for them."

"Of course," Dusty said, reaching into her jacket pocket and handing Bud the check for Howie.

"They're very excited to be able to play here, Dusty, so thanks for making that happen," Bud replied.

Now Dusty shifted in her seat, leaning toward Bud, her long flowery dress catching the sun where silver threads formed little stars around the flowers.

"Bud, I need your help. I know you already told me no, but I'm begging you this time. I have a check for $10,000 right here in my pocket, and I'm prepared to hand it to you right now, the only string attached being that you help me."

Bud replied, "Dusty, you know I'm dedicated to solving your sister's murder, but I can't take money for it, even though my wife's pressuring me to so she can buy an Airstream trailer for a spare bedroom. If I take pay, it makes me a professional P.I., which I'm not and would rather not be. We already talked about this."

"It's different now," she said, visibly disturbed. "Look, yesterday some guys from the Colorado Bureau of Investigation came here and went through Callie's wing, then confiscated all her private papers from Gene's office here in the castle."

"Did they have a warrant?" Bud asked.

"Yes, they showed it to Gene. They basically took everything. But they're not going to find anything, because Gene and I already went through all her papers."

"You did?" Bud was instantly on alert. Were Dusty and Gene trying to make sure there was nothing there that would implicate them?

"We've gone through everything in this castle, except in her wing, of course, since that's sealed off. The sheriff told us to stay out of there no matter what, so we are."

"You could be implicated if you did go in there," Bud replied, "Even if you left just one fingerprint."

"I think I'm already implicated," Dusty said. "That's why I need your help. I think I'm being set up."

Bud was surprised. "Set up? How?"

Dusty leaned over even further and whispered, "Callie kept a diary. She told me about it. She's kept diaries since she was a kid, but she told me she was going to use the material in this one to write a book."

A robin landed on the nearby lattice, and Dusty paused to watch it for a moment, then continued, not noticing the look of concern on Bud's face.

"Callie had been seeing someone, though she wouldn't tell me who, and she said she was finally truly happy for the first time. She wanted to hire a ghost writer and tell her story as a lesson to others that money doesn't buy happiness, love does."

"Sounds interesting," Bud commented.

"That diary is now missing," Dusty added. "I know exactly where she kept it, and the CBI guys said it wasn't there. Someone went into her room after she was killed and stole it, or maybe when they killed her. I told the CBI about it and they looked all over. I know Juno took it, I just know it somehow."

"But how is that setting you up?" Bud asked. "Was there something in it about you?"

"I don't know, but if there was, it wasn't anything I should worry about. But I know Juno took it, and I know he killed Callie. He had complete access to the castle. There was no evidence of someone breaking in. It had to be him. He lived right here, in a little wing off the back. And given what he said about seeing blood on her forehead, I don't understand why they haven't arrested him yet."

"These things take time," Bud replied.

"And I think Juno's the one trying to set me up."

"How so?"

Bud was beginning to think of Howie and how difficult it sometimes was getting information from him. He reached for the beads around his neck and began rolling them in his hand, waiting for Dusty to respond.

Finally, Dusty said, "I got a call from Sheriff Mason today. He interrogated me once, which was almost more than I could bear, them thinking I could kill my own sister. And now he wants me to come to Aspen so he can ask even more questions. He said primarily about her finances."

Bud asked, "Who's the executor of Callie's estate?"

"Her attorney down valley in Glenwood Springs," Dusty replied. "And I'm her only heir. I'm worried sick people will think I killed her to get her money. Callie was always ready to give me money, sometimes I didn't even ask. She was generous. I had no need to kill her for money."

Bud said, "Do you have access to her financial statements?"

Dusty looked pale, then looked around somewhat furtively. "No, but Gene does. He asked me to marry him a few months before Callie died. I told him I'd think about it, and now he's been pressing me even more. He said he has an incurable illness and wants to be with me while he still can. He even bought me a diamond, but I have no intention of accepting it. Once things clear and I have Callie's estate, I'm going to fire him. I don't trust him one bit. He very well could be the one setting me up. Callie told me when she hired him that he'd been arrested for being part of some multi-level marketing scheme. He convinced her that he was innocent, though."

Bud thought of the hounds tracking Callie's scent to Gene's car. He asked, "Did Callie ever ride in Gene's BMW?"

"No, not that I knew of. She hated anything that would set her apart from regular people, and even a BMW was too fancy for her. She drove a little Honda, though she does have her 1964 Olds convertible, but she used it only for special occasions."

"And yet she lived in a castle?"

"She bought this mansion because of its seclusion. She wasn't into having people hassling her, which they did when she lived in Aspen. I can't wait to sell it."

Bud now thought he would try again. "How are you being set up?"

Dusty sighed. "I want to hire you as a body guard. Twice now, someone's been messing around here after dark. I keep the gate closed and the security lights on, but they seem to be able to slip through it all. It's like they know where everything is and how to get around all the security. It has to be either Juno or Gene."

She continued, "And probably that same person left what is possibly the murder weapon in my car. I didn't lock the car doors, no need to out here, or so I thought, but yesterday morning when I went out there, there it was, on my front seat. I called Sheriff Mason and he sent a Deputy Schofield out to get it."

"What was it?"

"A piece of metal gutter with dried blood all over it. I believe it's the murder weapon. And if that's not a setup, I don't know what is."

# 30

Bud sat in a stuffy room in the basement of the Pitkin County Courthouse, wearing plastic gloves and straining to read the straightforward yet small handwriting in Callie Jensen's diary.

He had earlier declined Dusty's offer to be her body guard, telling her she needed someone full-time who could stay there at the castle, probably one of Mason's ex-deputies.

Thinking of Mason had prompted Bud to try his luck and see if the sheriff would let him take a look at Callie's diary, especially since he'd been the one responsible for it now being in their possession.

Mason had been curt with Bud, yet had also said he could examine it if he promised to share anything of importance with him, as Mason's office hadn't had a chance to take a look yet. He'd mentioned something about several officers being on a chase after a local dogsled kennel accidentally let their dogs out.

Bud leaned back in the chair, trying to get comfortable. He opened the small book and began reading entries penned several weeks before the murder.

*Juno told me he'd sat up all night in the bushes, waiting for the ghost to appear, but saw nothing. I was told when I bought this place that the Lion of Redstone haunted it, but this ghost is not male, it's female.*

Bud sighed, put the diary down, and pulled his cell phone from his pocket. He dialed Wilma Jean, who had come with him to Aspen and was now touring the Aspen Art Museum while he was in the courthouse.

"Hi hon," she answered. "You should see this display here. It's something else."

"What is it?" Bud asked.

"It's a bunch of sculptures by some Brazilian artist, and it's pretty wild. Here's what the brochure says: "Using stretchy, semitransparent fabric, aromatic spices, and crochet, these installations have an organic, biomorphic character that evokes a magical sense of space.'"

"Do they?" Bud asked.

"Do they what?"

"You know, evoke all that."

"Oh, well, not really," Wilma Jean laughed. "It's actually more evocative of someone who has too much time and money on their hands and is just a little wacky. But what's up?"

"Mason let me in to check out the diary. I just started, and I already have a question. Do you have any idea who the Lion of Redstone could be?"

Wilma Jean replied, "From what I've heard, that's what they called John Osgood, you know, the industrialist who built the town."

Bud answered, "Of course, makes sense. OK, next question. How can a ghost be male or female?"

Wilma Jean thought for a minute, then said, "When they were alive, they were obviously a man or woman, so now, even though they're just a spirit, they keep that appearance. What in the world is in that diary?"

"I don't know. I just got started," Bud said.

"OK," Wilma Jean replied. "I'll call you when I'm done here, unless you call me first."

"That's a plan," Bud replied, hanging up and returning to the diary.

*Hannah told me that Osgood died here at the castle in 1926, right in the bedroom I'm using. I'm going to move into the other wing. She said his ashes were supposedly scattered throughout the Crystal River Valley, but she's read where someone said they were scattered here in the garden right off the bedroom. I know it shouldn't bother me, but thinking he haunts this place gives me the creeps, especially given what I saw the other night. I'm thinking I may put it up for sale and move down valley. There's a nice ranch for sale out by Rifle.*

Bud continued reading, though most of the entries talked about more mundane things, like books she was reading (Zane Gray's "Riders of the Purple Sage") or what her friends were doing.

One entry in particular caught Bud's eye:

*I can't believe how hard it's getting for me to write songs any more. I seem to have lost my creative spark. The last one I wrote was, "Remember Folks, We're All Just Walking Each Other Home," and it wasn't one of my best, even though it did well. I think this ghost thing is getting to me.*

Bud kind of recalled hearing that song on the radio one evening when he and Howie were on their way to the old Green River Missile Base to check out Howie's metal detector. It had a catchy tune, if he recalled correctly. He now began wondering what Howie was doing. He needed to call him.

He continued reading, and things now took on a different tenor.

*I can't believe X is so hesitant to make our relationship public. His secretiveness bothers me.*

Bud was now wondering who this "X" was and whether or not "secretiveness" was really a word. He read on.

*X came over tonight and we had a nice long discussion about things. He says I'm too serious and need to just relax instead of always worrying about the future. Our time together makes me feel a bit better about my blundering attempts at enjoying my life rather than making something of it. He has such a high stress job, and I keep telling him to quit, but he feels some kind of obligation to his constituents.*

Bud was now up to the day before the murder, and he had yet to see any real clue as to who might want to kill Calico Callie, until he read an entry that said:

*I had a bit of a run-in with Gene today. It seems he and Dusty are getting close, and I really don't want to see him get involved with her. None of my business, but too close to home. I'm thinking of replacing him soon, then what they do will be of no concern to me. X says it's bad to mix family and business.*

Bud thought of the hounds going directly to Gene's BMW when Sprocket let them out. He was now to the end of the diary and Callie's last entry.

*Need to tell Juno to feed the squirrels and magpies more, as I saw a magpie trying to peck at the squirrel's tail for eating the nuts and apples. No need to fight over things. Last night I swore the ghost came into my room, but maybe it was a dream. Too vague to know for sure, but I'm terrified and plan on staying at the Inn tonight.*

Bud closed the book, wondering why Callie had changed her mind and stayed instead at the castle. He placed the diary back into its evidence box, removed the plastic gloves, got up, and opened the door.

He had one last stop to make before joining Wilma Jean for lunch. He had a hunch Mr. X might be someone with a high profile here in Aspen, someone with a public job, since he had constituents. If he was right, Sheriff Mason might be able to shed some light on things.

He headed up the stairs to Mason's office, trying not to think too much about how he had to stop and catch his breath a little more often than he would like and how maybe Wilma Jean was right about going on a diet—or maybe it was the altitude.

He would think about that later. Right now, he had bigger fish to fry.

## 31

Sheriff Mason sat across from Bud, leaning forward, elbows resting on his big oak desk. Bud noted an autographed picture of John Denver on his wall.

Seeing his interest, Mason said, "John and I got to know each other a bit, mostly from my deputies having to run off overzealous fans. I remember one time when he and I were sitting on the deck of the Cloud Nine Restaurant—that's out at the Aspen Highlands ski area—and some of the ski patrol thought it would be fun to jump over the deck. They launched off the side of the hill above the restaurant and floated about 20 feet above everyone, raining snow down on us, then landed on the other side."

He grinned with the memory, then continued, "It was the start of a long tradition, until the ski area's insurer, Lloyd's of London, shut it down. John thought it was pretty funny when one of the patrollers decided to launch off with his rescue toboggan in tow. It was something seeing this guy pulling a sled fly over your head. John told me later that was where he got the inspiration for his song, 'Fly Away.'"

Bud nodded, thinking that maybe he'd heard the song once or twice—probably down at Wilma Jean's bowling alley in Green River, Tumbleweed Bowl.

He thought he recalled it playing that time Raphie Tucker had accidentally let loose of his ball and it had gone through the window and rolled on down the street, not stopping until it hit the gutter several blocks away, giving a new meaning to the definition of "gutter ball."

Sheriff Mason stood and refilled his coffee cup from a small pot on the windowsill, offering Bud some. Bud declined, knowing he would soon have lunch. Besides, it smelled bitter and overboiled, now that he'd become a bit of a coffee connoisseur, thanks to Wilma Jean, who always bought Jamaican Blue Mountain coffee.

Mason sat back down and leaned back, then said in a serious voice, "Bud, I'm sorry, but I can't answer any questions because I'm no longer on the case."

Bud was surprised. "How can the sheriff of the county a murder was committed in no longer be on the case?"

Mason answered, "It's a conflict of interest. I should have never been on it in the first place, but I didn't want to admit what was going on. I'll probably lose my job over it before it's all over."

"I'm sorry to hear that," Bud replied. He waited, knowing Mason would tell him more only if he wanted. It really was none of his business, unless it somehow related to Callie's murder.

Finally, Mason said, "I may as well tell you since it's already all over town. I was having an affair with Calico Callie."

"An affair?" Bud was shocked. It was about the last thing he expected to hear. He thought that maybe Mason could shed some light on who Mr. X was, but he hadn't expected him to actually *be* Mr. X.

"Yeah, we started seeing each other after a big benefit we were both asked to host. It seemed innocent enough, since we both have a big heart for adopted kids."

"A benefit?" Bud asked lamely, still in shock.

"Yeah, Aspen is big on benefits, and if you can get some celebrity or someone well-known to host it, you're guaranteed you'll do well. So, this organization for adopted kids asked us both. Callie and I met several times to get everything ready, and we just really clicked. I can't tell you how rough her death has been on me personally."

Bud asked, "Can I ask, I mean, it's none of my business, but what does your wife think of all this?"

"My wife? I'm not married. Been divorced some five or more years."

Bud paused. "Sheriff Mason, you were having a relationship, not an affair. Most people think of an affair as when you're doing something you shouldn't, like if you're married. There's nothing wrong with having a relationship, last I heard. Anyway, that's how I've always understood it."

Sheriff Mason was silent. He then said, "Well, whatever it was, I miss her. Did you know she was adopted?"

"No, I didn't know that. Was Dusty her adopted sister then?"

"Yeah, Dusty's mom and dad adopted Callie when she was three years old. He was an aeronautical engineer for Boeing in Seattle. Callie grew up in a pretty urban environment, yet she was different from the start, at least so she told me. She was never interested in the things Dusty was. Callie always wanted to be with horses or animals and wanted to be out in the country. It's almost like it was genetic, and her parents didn't understand her at all. She became a country singer out of love for country, not to get rich. She was authentic, and people recognized that and liked her for it."

"So, she and Dusty didn't have much in common, it sounds like. Was Dusty ever resentful of Callie's success, or do you know?"

"Callie never mentioned it, but we never saw much of Dusty. She was too busy globetrotting with the guy who's now her ex-husband. He was a doctor here in Aspen, and Dusty was pretty shook up when he filed for a divorce. She went from being affluent to being just regular people like you and me. Callie did say she was always asking her for money, which Callie always gave her. She was generous like that."

Now Mason paused again. Finally, he said, "Listen, Bud, I know you're the real deal and won't tell anyone where you got this information. I'm probably going to be fired anyway, and you seem like the only one who's really doing much on this case. The CBI was out at the castle yesterday and did a thorough search of Callie's apartment. I already had a deputy look around out there, but they wanted to go through it again."

He stopped for a moment as someone began talking on Mason's intercom, saying, "Sheriff, Councilman Thomas is waiting in the Council Room."

"I need to go, but Bud," Mason said thoughtfully, "You need to know that I've had my detectives do a search through Callie's phone and bank statements, her bank box, and anything else we could think of. We haven't found anything irregular. I don't think her sister had anything to do with the murder, though I wondered at first. Her business manager had no motive, that I can see. That's all I can tell you right now."

Bud replied, "I know you need to go, but did you send the piece of gutter found in Dusty's car to the lab?"

Mason answered, "Yes, it's at the lab. I'll let you know when the results come back, but it fits the description of the weapon the coroner said killed Callie. Let's stay in touch."

"No problem," Bud replied. "But I really need one thing to help me with all this—your permission to search through Callie's private quarters at the castle."

Mason said, "You have my permission. I'll make sure everyone knows."

The sheriff then added, "And say, let me know if you see a locket anywhere. Callie always wore a locket with a photo of her and her brother as children with their grandfather. It meant a lot to her, and it was missing after the murder. She wore it day and night, so someone had to have taken it off her. Both my detective and the CBI did a thorough search of her room, and it's just not there. It would implicate whoever has it. Gotta go. I know I'm about to get fired, so wish me luck. And thanks for all you're doing."

Mason stood up to leave, shook Bud's hand, then the two of them walked out into the hall, Mason going up the stairs while Bud walked out the front door.

Bud stood there for a moment, wondering what Mason had meant by "thanks for all you're doing." For some reason, he didn't feel like he'd been doing much of anything, and he felt he was no closer to solving the Calico Callie murder than when he'd first arrived.

## 32

Bud and Wilma Jean had just finished their lunch at the Ice House Cafe, Bud having ordered a fish sandwich. He rarely ate fish, as it was hard to get fresh fish in Green River, unless one enjoyed river carp, which was a bit bony, in Bud's opinion, and one had to catch it themselves.

They had initially stopped for lunch at a little bistro in Aspen, but when Wilma Jean saw the prices, she'd made an executive decision that they would return to Redstone to eat. Besides, even though it was a nice cool day, they decided the dogs had been in the car long enough. They would drop them off at the cottage, then go eat.

The Ice House had decent food, and the fish sandwich wasn't bad, though Bud knew it was far from what he would get in some little coastal town like Seaside, Oregon, which he'd once visited long ago on a lark with his buddies after graduating high school.

Hannah interrupted Bud's train of thought, thereby saving it from being derailed by nostalgia, asking if they'd like some ice cream for dessert. Bud noted that she looked haggard and tired, as if she'd been up all night.

They ordered homemade strawberry ice cream, then Bud asked, "Hannah, you feeling OK? You look kind of tired today."

Hannah replied, "I don't know why, but I just can't seem to get rested up. Ever since the murder, I can't seem to sleep well. I can't wait to get out of here."

"Where will you go?" asked Wilma Jean with concern.

"I don't know exactly, but I have a niece in Oregon. She said I could come up there until I figured things out."

"Seaside?" Bud asked.

"How did you know?" Hannah asked suspiciously.

"Just a guess," Bud replied. "I was just thinking about the fresh fish I ate there once when I was younger. Just a coincidence."

Hannah picked up their lunch dishes and carried them back into the kitchen, turning to give Bud another suspicious look.

Just then, Wilma Jean's phone rang. Bud half-listened in on her conversation as he studied the menu to see if there were any other fish dishes on it.

"Maureen?" Wilma Jean paused, and Bud could now hear someone talking so loud he could almost make out what they were saying.

Wilma Jean finally said, "You're kidding, right? I mean, Old Man Green, of all people? And now they're looking for Howie? I find that hard to believe. Look, don't cry, sweetheart, I'll put Bud on, and he can figure out exactly what to do. I know he'll have a solution, so just hang on there."

She handed Bud the phone and whispered, "Maureen says Old Man Green just got arrested, and now they're looking for Howie."

"Who is?" Bud asked, taking the phone just as Hannah brought two dishes of strawberry ice cream with chocolate sprinkles on top.

He answered the phone. "Maureen, what's going on?"

He strained to hear, but all he could make out was sobbing. Finally, Maureen said, "They just arrested Old Man Green, and they came here to the cafe, looking for Howie. He's not at the office, so I think he's out on patrol. They said they were going to arrest him."

Bud groaned. He had no idea why anyone would want to arrest the Sheriff of Emery County, but he now wondered if it weren't related to Howie's late nights and the possible drinking Maureen had complained about earlier.

"Who is it?" Bud asked.

"Old Man Green and Howie," Maureen said, her voice cracking.

"No, I mean, who arrested Old Man Green?"

"They said they're from the Department of Public Safety," Maureen answered.

"Everything related to law-enforcement in Utah comes through that department, Maureen. Did they say what division they were with?"

She replied, "The Bureau of Criminal Investigation. When I told them I was his wife, they said he was wanted for illegal alcohol manufacturing and sales."

"Bootlegging," Bud replied grimly. "This will be hard on his run for election as sheriff—in fact, probably a disaster. After all, this is Utah, home of strict liquor laws. I know Howie didn't do anything illegal, because that's not our Howie. And Old Man Green's such a straight shooter he would shoot himself before he broke the law."

Hannah was now standing by Bud, taking it all in, which irritated Bud to no end.

He whispered to Maureen, "Have you tried calling Howie?"

"He's not answering. He might be down at the highway shop where Barry our bass player works. He sometimes stops down there to talk about the band and stuff like that."

Bud thought for a minute, then said, "Look, see if you can find Howie before they do. Have one of Krider's girls come down and watch the cafe for a bit and go run around and look for him. Even if he's innocent, getting arrested will end his law-enforcement career. People won't care that he's innocent."

"I can't imagine what he's been up to," Maureen sobbed. "OK, I'm going to go find him. I'll call you if I can figure out where he is."

Bud hung up the phone, noticing his ice cream was melting, but he no longer had an appetite for anything.

Hannah was now gone.

"Hannah is acting very strange," Wilma Jean said quietly.

"How so?" Bud asked. "I mean, other than always eavesdropping on everyone."

"She has a strange look about her. It's hard to explain, like she's very distracted. She said she was going upstairs to get something that belongs to me. She can't possibly have anything of mine, Bud. I just want to leave."

Bud put enough money on the table to cover their bill and a tip, then he and Wilma Jean quickly walked out the door and were soon back to their little rental cottage.

They slipped through the door, the dogs greeting them and wagging their tails, acting like they'd been abandoned forever, even though it had only been an hour. Bud turned, looked toward the Ice House Cafe, then locked the door and closed the curtains.

# 33

Bud and Doc Richardson sat on the back veranda of the cottage, Bud with the dogs sleeping in his lap and Doc leafing through a glossy magazine extolling the many excellent tourist activities of the Crystal Valley—four-wheeling, photography, fine dining, hiking, strolling the boulevard, and touring the marble quarry. Bud had looked through it earlier and noted there was no mention of the numerous bears, ghosts, and early winter snows, not to mention celebrity murders.

"Thanks for dinner," Doc said to Bud, who was thinking he should get up and get his camera and see if he could capture the way the rose-colored clouds reflected in the river. He leaned back, deciding to just enjoy the show, as it was too much trouble to make the dogs get down.

Bud replied, "That's our first time at the Redstone Inn. Lots of history there, and the food was good, too."

"Not bad," Doc replied. "Wilma Jean said you guys will soon be leaving for Radium. How's the detective work going? You think you'll be able to figure it all out before you leave?"

Bud shrugged his shoulders. "I don't know. It seems like I just think I'm on the right track and something new comes up. It's pretty frustrating, and I'm about ready to call it quits and let the experts solve it."

"The Pitkin County Sheriff's Office?" Doc asked.

"Them and the Colorado Bureau of Investigation. It's actually their job, not mine."

"Bud," Doc said quietly, "I still haven't figured out why you would come here and get all involved in trying to solve the murder of someone you didn't even know. It would be different if you were on someone's payroll or something."

Bud answered, "Well, Doc, I've spent way too much time trying to figure that out myself, and I have no idea. It's almost like a compulsion. I think maybe it has something to do with Wilma Jean. This gal looked enough like her to be her sister, and I think that's tugging at me."

Doc put his magazine aside. "Well, I certainly can understand that. But this is supposed to be a vacation. Seems to me you just aren't too good at kicking back and doing nothing. I'm the same way myself. Even though I'm retired, I find I need something to keep me going every day. That's why I started the peach orchard there in Palisade, even though it's going to be years before it really starts to produce."

"I'm a bit jealous, Doc, but at least I can go work on Krider's Farm part of the time. I want to put in a watermelon patch on our two acres one of these days, but at the rate I'm going, it won't be until I retire, and that's a ways off."

"Any news on where Howie is?" Doc asked.

"No idea. Haven't heard a word from Maureen. She said she'd call when she found him. I'm actually pretty worried and may end up going on back over there."

"By the way, Bud," Doc replied. "You were telling me about this guy named Juno and how you and the deputy followed him out of the high country right before the big snow. Did you ever find out if he came out or not?"

Bud sighed. "Chuck called me and told me he'd gone back in there after everything melted off and Juno's car was gone, so I assume Juno got out OK. But say, were you ever able to get ahold of Judge

Richter? I know you guys were friends when you were practicing in Price and were coroner. Did he say anything about why they were looking for Howie?"

Doc replied, "Well, I did talk to Richter. He said an investigator from Salt Lake had come in and asked for a search warrant, but he denied it. Said they didn't have enough evidence. Apparently, they said that they'd received a tip that Old Man Green was brewing alcohol in his barn and selling it. There's nothing illegal about making your own brew, but it's illegal to sell it without the proper licensing."

"How in hellsbells did they figure that out?" Bud asked.

"I guess there was some other fellow involved, and he was the one doing the actual selling. They haven't been able to track him down yet, but someone ratted him out."

"Doesn't sound like much of case to me, but if Howie gets arrested, that will be the end of his career as sheriff, even if they drop the case. People forget the not guilty part and focus on the arrest, especially during an election year."

Doc said, "Richter said they were making watermelon spritzers. I guess they arrested Old Man Green and he confessed. But he said they weren't selling it, just experimenting. They wanted to get it down right and then apply for a license and get an investor and sell the stuff. They were going to call it 'Old Man Green's Watermelon Elixir.'"

"Is he in jail?" Bud asked with concern.

"No, they let him go on a personal recognizance. I mean, the old guy's got to be in his 80s. He's never done anything wrong, and this is probably killing him. It's not illegal to brew your own, not even in Utah. That's why Richter wouldn't give them a search warrant."

Bud tried to tip his wicker chair back, forgetting once again how heavy it was and skidding it back, waking the dogs.

He said, "I think this may solve the mystery of Howie's so-called drinking problem, Doc. Maureen's been upset because he's come home a few times drunk and doesn't even remember it the next day. I have a feeling Old Man Green's been using him as a guinea pig and

Howie doesn't even know it—Green's own private Watermelon Elixir taster. And I just bet Howie's Land Cruiser wasn't even stolen. Howie was probably drunk and forgot he parked it behind the barn."

"I would think Howie wouldn't have much resistance to a bit of alcohol," Doc replied. "He doesn't strike me as someone with much experience in that subject."

"And it would be a real shame if he lost his job over it," Bud added, just as his phone rang.

"It's Maureen," he said, looking at the caller ID.

"Yell-ow," he answered.

He was silent for awhile, listening, then finally said, "OK. Good work, Maureen. You just keep him out there for the night. Doc Richardson's here, and don't you worry, between the two of us, we'll figure something out."

He hung up and turned to Doc. "She found him out at the old Missile Base messing around with his metal detector. He's going to camp out there tonight. She said he was pretty upset when he found out what was going on and wanted to turn himself in, even though he couldn't figure out what he'd done wrong. Doc, I bet Old Man Green probably doesn't even realize Howie has no immunity to alcohol."

The pair sat silently, listening to the river, when Bud's phone rang again. It was Maureen.

"Bud, I don't know what to do," she said glumly. "Howie's going home. He says he's going to turn himself in first thing in the morning."

She paused, then added, "You might as well tell the gal at the castle that Howie and the Ramblin' Road Rangers won't be there for her big party, because the band leader will be in jail."

## 34

Bud sat yet again in the back booth of the Ice House Cafe, waiting for Hannah to bring him a cup of coffee. Wilma Jean had gone with Millie to soak in the big hot springs pool down valley in Glenwood Springs, and Doc had wandered across the highway to inspect the old coke ovens.

Hannah brought Bud his coffee and a small dish of vanilla ice cream and sat down across from him. She seemed to be a little more rested than the previous day, when he and Wilma Jean had both thought she seemed a bit off.

"So, you guys are probably going to be leaving soon, huh?" she asked.

"Yes, we're down to our last week."

"Are you going to the big party at the castle? I was invited, but that place gives me the creeps."

"I don't know if we're going or not at this point, Hannah. Some friends of ours were supposed to play for it, but if they don't make it, we may leave Redstone early."

Bud recalled what Hannah had said the previous day and asked, "Say, didn't you say yesterday that you had something upstairs that belonged to my wife?"

"I said that? I don't know why I would say that. Are you sure I said that?"

Bud decided to let it go. "I must have been mistaken."

It seemed like Hannah was in a more tractable mood than the previous day, so he asked, "Say, Hannah, do you know where Juno is?"

"No," she replied bluntly.

"You do realize that, if you do know, you can be arrested for obstructing justice. There's an arrest warrant out for him. Are you sure you don't know where he is, Hannah?"

"I know where he was, but I'm not sure where he is now."

"Where was he?"

"He went up to Lead King Basin for awhile, like I told you, but the weather turned and he came back out. I haven't seen him since then. There's a rumor that he's been hanging out with the woman with the ice-cream truck up in Marble."

Bud made a note to himself. He would have to call Deputy Schofield and see if he was aware of this.

He now tried again. "Hannah, did Juno kill Callie?"

"No."

"Then why won't he turn himself in? If he's innocent, he can clear things up and forget all this."

She replied, "Because he knows who killed her, and he knows the sheriff will make him confess."

"Why doesn't he want to tell?"

"I don't know—well, I do know. He told me it's a close friend, someone he knows, and the last thing he's gonna do is get them in trouble."

"But they already got themselves in trouble, Hannah. If they killed Callie, they're responsible. Juno doesn't have the right to play judge and jury."

"He thinks he does. He says it's a special case."

"What else did he tell you?"

"Nothing."

Now Hannah noticed something out the front window. She stood to get a better view.

"Here comes Gus Dearhammer. I should eighty-six the old goat from the cafe."

"Why?" Bud asked.

"He used to go over and hang out with Callie. He talked her into grubstaking him for a silver mine up in the basin. He and Juno used to be friends, but this really made Juno mad."

"Why?"

"Because Juno wanted to do his own prospecting, but he could never get up enough money to do it."

"Why didn't he ask Callie?"

"He was too proud. He didn't want to ask."

"But Callie surely wouldn't have minded, especially if she grubstaked Gus."

"Juno was very protective of Callie and tried his best to look out for her, but she wouldn't always listen to him. He would never have asked her for money. That's why it's so ironic that they think he killed her. He didn't have it in him."

"But why are *you* mad at Gus?"

"Juno used to go up to Lead King and check up on him, make sure he was really doing what he said he was with Callie's money. This made Gus mad, and he and Juno finally had a falling out. I'm mad because Juno's mad."

"I see," Bud replied as Gus and Sprocket walked in. They sat down, and Hannah handed them menus, not saying a word, then retreated into the kitchen.

Bud nodded at the pair, sipping his coffee, then pulled his cell phone from his pocket. He dialed the Emery County Sheriff's Office, but no one answered. He then dialed Howie's cell phone, and again no answer. He tried the Melon Rind Cafe, and one of Krider's daughters answered, saying she hadn't seen Howie nor Maureen since the day before.

Bud was now genuinely worried, and he toyed with the idea of asking Doc Richardson to drive him over to Green River to see what was going on. He fiddled with the beads around his neck, then decided if he hadn't been able to get ahold of anyone by early after-noon, he would ask Doc for a ride.

In the meantime, Wilma Jean could be packing their stuff and could then take Millie to their house in Palisade and come on over to Green River herself. Her ankle was now fine and she would have no trouble driving that far.

Bud was worried about Howie, but he now felt somewhat reluc-tant to leave. Maybe it was simply the fact that he was becoming familiar with the area and had met a few people, but he also knew it was because something was simmering in the back of his subcon-scious—he knew somehow that he had the clues he needed to solve Callie's murder, yet he just couldn't put them together. If he left now, he knew things would never come together, and if Callie's murder were solved, it wouldn't be by him.

Gus and Sprocket had placed their order, and Bud could now see Doc walking down the boulevard, coming his way. He finished his coffee, placed his napkin on the table, and as he was putting on his straw cowboy hat, noticed a piece of paper stuck into its brim.

How had someone managed to put a piece of paper there without him seeing them? He always had his hat with him everywhere he went. Someone had to have done it during the brief moment he'd gone into the restroom to wash his hands.

He carefully unfolded the note. Scribbled in large letters in what appeared to be someone's attempt at disguising their handwriting were the words:

*Stop looking in the wrong places. Everyone knows the zombie killed Callie.*

# 35

Bud wandered along the edge of the river, not far from the cottage, letting the dogs run a bit and get their feet wet in the icy water. The river had risen just a little, probably from snow melting up in the high country, Bud figured, as things had warmed up since that last storm.

Doc Richardson was taking a nap, the gals were still in Glenwood Springs, and Bud was enjoying having some time to himself. It was the only way he could get any thinking done, and the Calico Callie case was beginning to feel like being on a merry-go-round, one with no way to jump off.

He felt like he was beginning to lose track of everything, and being alone to think would maybe let him put the loose ends together, assuming he could recall them all.

He picked up a stick and threw it to Hoppie, who promptly missed the toss and ran after it into the shallow water near the bank, getting himself soaking wet as he watched the stick float on down beyond his reach. Bud loved Bassets, but he had to concede they weren't the fastest dogs on the block, as their long stocky bodies were obviously not built for speed.

Bud picked up another stick and promptly began dragging it in the sand as they walked along. He was oblivious to little Pierre, who was trying to grab it but kept missing. Now deep in thought, Bus was thinking about Juno Alaska.

It seemed like all roads led to Juno, and even the Pitkin County Sheriff's Department seemed to think he was the murderer. But Hannah was sure he wasn't, and Bud didn't think she was just trying to protect him.

Bud recalled another murder he'd been working on back when he was still Sheriff of Emery County, one that had him just as stymied. It was before he'd taken the job at Krider's farm, and he'd asked Professor Krider for his advice. Krider was a well-known mystery writer and had researched lots of cases for his plots, so Bud hoped he could provide some new insight.

Krider had told Bud to look for the person who had the most to lose in a murder case, as they would be the one most scared and thereby most likely to make a mistake. His words had helped Bud solve the case.

Bud now sat on a rock, little Pierre finally grabbing onto the end of the stick and growling as he tried to shake it. He thought about Juno and what motives he might have to murder Callie Jensen.

It just didn't make sense. Of all people, Juno would be the most affected by her death, as he stood to lose not only his job, but also his home. He would be the least likely one to want her dead, unless there was something going on that Bud wasn't aware of.

Bud now recalled the rest of his conversation with Krider. After telling Krider who he thought the murderer was, Krider had said, "Be careful. Things aren't always what they seem."

Of course, Krider was right, and Bud had been *way* off track, even though he had managed to finally figure it all out. That innocent suspect had been Doc Richardson, who was now one of Bud's best friends. Bud had been way off track, even though all roads led to Doc at the time.

But Bud had learned that sometimes solutions required thinking outside the box, and suspecting Juno just seemed too obvious, especially after he'd called 911 and said he'd seen blood on Callie's forehead, something that would be possible only if he'd been there when she was murdered.

But then, sometimes the obvious was the correct solution. If Juno had seen blood on her forehead, he had to have been involved. But why call 911 and implicate oneself? Once again, it just didn't make sense.

Bud again began walking down the riverbank, dragging the stick behind him, Pierre hanging on and Hoppie nipping at his heels.

What about Dusty and Callie's business manager, Gene? Dusty really had no reason to kill Callie that Bud knew, especially since she'd said Callie had been generous to her when it came to money. If Dusty could get money whenever she asked, why kill her benefactor? Or maybe Dusty was tired of asking and knew, as Callie's only relative, she would inherit her estate and would have all the money she needed without having to ask.

Bud thought back again. Before Millie had married Doc and was still running the Ghost Rock Cafe up on the Swell above Green River, she had told Bud that, "When people are killed, there's either love or money involved."

Gene knew exactly how much money Callie had, and since he and Dusty were involved in some sort of blossoming relationship, he could have easily shared that information with Dusty. Callie hadn't been happy about their involvement, according to her diary. And what about the hounds tracking Callie's scent to Gene's BMW?

And what about Sheriff Mason himself? In Bud's mind, he wasn't much of a suspect, but maybe the fact that Mason was a law officer was getting in the way of Bud's objectivity. Lawmen weren't necessarily beyond breaking the law, and in some cases, they were harder to catch because of their knowledge of law enforcement techniques.

And what about Gus? Callie had loaned him money to work on his mine. Had they somehow got into a disagreement over that and he'd killed her? He lived nearby and could have easily just walked away. He and Juno were at odds—did Juno know something about Gus that Gus didn't want to get out? Was Juno's life in danger?

Bud paused, dropping the stick. They were now behind the Ice

House Cafe. Bud walked over to the big marble icicle sculpture, running his hands over the smooth texture of the stone.

No matter how he cut it, Juno still seemed to be the most obvious suspect. But how did Hannah fit in? She seemed to be very protective of Juno, yet she sometimes seemed frustrated with him. And her mood swings or whatever you wanted to call them seemed very odd to Bud, as well as the time she'd yelled out the window at him. And he was pretty sure she'd been the one who'd left the note saying the zombie had killed Callie.

Of course, he figured she'd meant Wilma Jean, since she'd referred to her as the zombie before—or had she? Bud tried to think back. Had Callie ever actually called Wilma Jean a zombie?

He recalled the TV announcer saying a zombie had been sighted in Redstone after Callie's death, and of course he had to be referring to Wilma Jean, who had then said she didn't want to stay if everyone thought she was a zombie.

And Hannah had yelled out the stuff about blood everywhere, saying the zombie would pay with her life, but had she actually called Wilma Jean the zombie?

Bud now stopped, frozen in his tracks. How could he be so oblivious? There wasn't one time he could think of that Hannah had actually called Wilma Jean a zombie—he'd just been presumptuous. She had to be referring to someone else. It was a major clue, and he'd totally missed it.

He now thought back to what she'd yelled out that early morning from her window. He'd written it down, it had been so strange.

He pulled a small notebook from his pocket.

*There's blood everywhere, Mr. Shumway. Blood on the forehead. Blood on the headboard. Blood on the moon and blood on the Unknown's Tomb. The zombie will pay, she'll pay with her life.*

Bud started back toward the cottage. He was disappointed in himself. He had completely overlooked what could be important clues in solving Callie's murder.

Hannah obviously knew something, and he intended to find out exactly what that something was.

## 36

It had warmed up, and Bud had put the dogs in the cottage. Seeing that Doc was still taking a nap, he decided to walk down the boulevard to the ice cream shop and get a strawberry cone. He would then go back and see if Doc was awake. He was worried about Howie and needed to talk to Doc about the best course of action.

Bud ordered the ice cream and sat down on a nearby bench when his phone rang. For once, he was very happy to see Howie's number on the caller ID. He had half expected to see the number for the Emery County Jail.

"Yell-ow," he answered.

"That you, Sheriff?" Howie asked.

"Howie, how's everything going? I'm sure glad to hear from you. Where are you?"

"Oh, I'm having lunch at the Chow Down. Where did you think I would be, in jail?"

"Well..."

"Guess who's buying me and Old Man Green lunch."

"Old Man Green's with you?"

"He is. He's sitting right here, and he just took his lower bridge out so he can eat. Seems to me it would do more good in. He says it cost so much he doesn't want to wear it out, but what good are false teeth if you don't use them?"

"OK, Howie. Who's buying you guys lunch?"

There was a long pause, and Bud could hear someone talking in the background, saying something about toothpaste. Finally, Howie came back on.

"Agents Millikin and Powers. And Bud, you'd never guess, but they've been telling me about how to polish up my badge. It's getting pretty tarnished. Did you know you can send it back to the company you bought it from and they'll refurbish it for free?"

Bud tried not to groan. "No, Howie, I didn't know that."

"I'm going to try using toothpaste first. Agent Powers says that works great."

"That's nice, Howie, but I thought they were out looking to arrest you. What happened?"

Bud could hear Howie saying something to the waitress about ice cream for his coffee. Finally, Howie replied, "Well, Sheriff, I decided it was wrong to be hiding out from the law, especially since I *am* the law. What kind of an example is that? I mean, if I have kids someday, do I want to tell them that, as a lawman, I was running from the law? It just doesn't make sense."

Bud tried to hide his impatience. "So, Howie, what did you do?"

"Well, I went home. Maureen wasn't real keen on that. I think it was the first time ever she was mad at me for *coming* home. But I figured hiding out wasn't good, so I went home, got a good night's rest, then went into the office the next morning."

"And then what?" Bud asked, hoping Howie wouldn't go into pause mode.

Howie continued, "Sheriff, life sure is puzzling sometimes. I was sitting there, reading one of my *Lost Treasure* magazines, when I got a call from this tourist down at the car wash. He was pretty mad, as he'd put four dollars in, and the water wouldn't come on. So, I drove down there and the two of us figured out that the water had been turned off. Probably some kids pulling a prank. I turned it back on, and all was well."

Bud sighed. He watched as a pair of tourists walked by, leading a big boxer. The dog stopped and sniffed Bud's pant cuffs, but the couple pulled him away, apologizing.

"It's OK," Bud said. "He just smells my dogs."

Howie asked, "What did you say?"

"Nothing, Howie. So what happened?"

"Well, I went back to the office and hung around, waiting to be arrested, but it just didn't look like it was going to happen, at least not on my schedule, so I decided to take a break and go down to the Chow Down and get a cup of coffee like I used to do with you when I was just a deputy."

"While I was there, I got a call from Mrs. Taylor saying she'd seen somebody down by the bridge who looked like they were in trouble. So, I got in the Land Cruiser and drove on down by the river, and I could make out some guy out on the beach a ways, yelling."

Bud held his breath, hoping Howie wouldn't stop. It was the most talking at once he figured he'd ever heard him do.

Howie continued, "Well, to make a long story short, or maybe a short story long, this guy down on the beach had found himself a patch of quicksand and was sinking."

"When I got there, he was clear up to his knees, and man, was he stuck. There's not much quicksand on the Green, it's not like the Colorado, but once in awhile you can find a patch if you look hard enough, and I guess this guy was itching for some adventure, because he was stucker than a jackrabbit in bentonite clay."

Howie laughed, then went on. "There was nothing I could do by myself, so I called Old Man Green, and he came right over with his old Allis Chalmers tractor. He had a cable, and I went out as far as I dared and tried to throw it out to this guy, but I just couldn't reach him. Before long, I could feel myself sinking, and man, that's a spooky feeling, I can tell you."

"I didn't know what to do to help this poor fellow, but then I remembered what my granddad had told me once when I was a little kid, all about quicksand. He said, 'Howie, if you're ever in quicksand, lie down and roll. It redistributes your weight and will give you traction.' So I yelled out to the guy to lie down and roll, but he wouldn't do it. He was too scared."

"Finally, he was in up to his thighs, and I told him if he didn't lie down and roll pretty soon, he'd be in too deep to do anything constructive, and he could start singing some religious tune, 'cause he would soon be meeting the angels. I suggested he try 'On Christ, The Solid Rock I Stand, All Other Ground is Sinking Sand,' or something like that."

"That got to him, and he finally leaned over and started rolling. He got over close to me and I grabbed him and pulled him out. He was white as a sheet, well, the part not covered with mud, which was pretty much only his face."

"Old Man Green gave us a ride on his tractor to his place, and we hosed ourselves down. I didn't want to get the Land Cruiser all messed up. It's almost impossible to get sand out of stuff."

"Anyway, while we were all waiting to dry, we took this guy into Old Man Green's barn and gave him some watermelon spritzer to wake him up a bit. He called his buddy, who had dropped him off at the river to go fishing, and when that guy showed up, that's when Old Man Green recognized them."

"It was the same guys who had arrested Old Man Green and were after me. Anyway, once they saw his operation there, they agreed it was pretty amateurish and wouldn't stand up in court. We told them we'd never sold anything."

"Did you ever find out who contacted them in the first place?" Bud asked.

"We did. It was Jerry Gruber's ex-wife. He was also involved in this little enterprise, in fact, he and Old Man Green were the main investors. I was just there to help out doing a few taste tests, though I don't remember much about that."

Howie continued. "You remember Jerry—he lives in Thompson Springs and is part of the Liar's Club up there. His wife divorced him years ago but refuses to move out. He traded one of his buddies some spritzer for $20, and she got word of it and called the Board of Alcohol up in Salt Lake. I think she feels kind of bad about it now, 'cause she told Jerry he's more of a gentleman when he drinks, and she hopes he keeps it up."

"So, Howie, does this mean you guys will still be coming over to play for the party? It's day after tomorrow."

"You bet," Howie answered, excited. "Krider's daughter's going to watch Bodie and Tobie for us. We're all pretty fired up to have our first paying gig."

"Great," Bud replied. "Say, if you look in my closet, you'll see a tweed jacket. Could you bring it with you?"

"Roger," Howie replied. "Will do."

"Oh, and hey," Bud added, thinking about Juno burying things in the meadow, "Bring your metal detector."

"Sure. That sounds good. Maybe we can go up to some of the old mine dumps," Howie replied enthusiastically.

Bud added, "I have something else in mind, but maybe that, too. But you remember Millie and Doc Richardson? They're here and maybe they can go to the party, if we can get an invite from Dusty."

"Sure, I remember them," Howie replied. "Doc's the one who took my tonsils out when I was 18. My parents put it off a bit. Tell him we'll play a song just for them."

"Will do," Bud replied. "And I can't tell you how happy I am to hear you're not in jail."

"Me, too," Howie replied, saying goodbye, leaving Bud wondering how his pant cuffs had managed to get a few yellow sprinkles on them—until he remembered the boxer.

# 37

Bud sat in the lounge of the Redstone Inn, laptop open, hoping he wouldn't see Hannah or anyone he knew, as he really wanted some time to focus on the research he needed to do. He'd decided to come to the Inn instead of the Ice House Cafe so he could have some privacy for once, with Hannah not peeking over his shoulder.

Doc had gone with Wilma Jean and Millie for a drive up the valley to see the fall colors, promising to return in time for dinner. Bud felt bad that he wasn't going, but he had something on his mind, something that wouldn't wait, and he was running out of time. The big memorial party was coming up, and he and Wilma Jean would be leaving shortly after that.

He wanted to do some research on ghosts.

He sat in the back corner of the big lounge, which was filled with comfy leather chairs and sofas and had the feel of a very quiet refuge with its big beveled glass windows looking out on the river. No one was there except him and an older couple in the other corner drinking tea and reading newspapers.

Bud got comfortable, then opened his laptop and connected to the Redstone Inn's wifi signal. He found the website for the *Salt Lake*

*Tribune*, checking to see if there was any news about Green River—there never was—or even southeast Utah.

The last real news story he'd seen about his part of the state was when some state officials had decided to raft the Green and afterwards ended up in Jay's Tavern, where they immediately got into a big fight over whether or not Kitty the waitress dyed her hair (according to Wilma Jean, she did).

Of course, that had been just an excuse to let off all the steam they'd accumulated while rafting and arguing over state policies about regulating the rafting industry.

Anyway, Bud remembered that story because he'd been the one called to break up the fight and had later received a thank-you note from the bunch for not throwing them in jail. The only reason he hadn't done so was because he didn't want to have to drive them over to the jail in Castle Dale while they were drunk, but he didn't tell them that.

An article linked to the *New York Times* now caught Bud's eye: "Fiddling Your Way to Fitness." He skimmed the article, which basically reported a study on people who fiddle, saying they tend to have better fitness levels than those who don't.

This piqued Bud's interest, and he did a search on "fiddling" to see what he would come up with.

One article asked if there was a biological reason people fiddled, then quoted a professor of psychology as saying, "The cognitive load hypothesis says we sometimes partly offload complex thoughts or problems into movement, thus freeing up our mental resources to devote to the solution."

Bud leaned back, smiling, fiddling with the beads around his neck. So, he thought, there is a reason for fiddling. He wasn't just being nervous, but really did need to fiddle to think more clearly.

He felt a bit vindicated, bookmarking the page to later show Wilma Jean. Maybe she would stop getting after him for fiddling after she read this.

Bud's phone rang. He could tell from the caller ID it was Sheriff Mason.

"Yell-ow," Bud answered quietly, so as not to disturb the couple across the room.

"Bud, Mason here. I'm still not on the case, but at least they haven't fired me yet. But I did just find out something I think you'll find interesting. The lab report came back on that piece of gutter found in Dusty's car. There are plenty of fingerprints, but not of anyone on file."

"Could they be Juno's?" Bud asked.

"They could," answered the sheriff. "And if we could find him and arrest him, we could verify that either way. But until then, we have no way of knowing. We do have Dusty and Gene's prints on file and they're nether of theirs. And the blood's the same deal—no idea whose it is. We do know it's not Callie's."

"Interesting," Bud replied. "So, the gutter wasn't the murder instrument, at least not for Callie's murder, since her blood's not on it."

"Are you thinking someone else was killed?" Mason asked.

"Well, not that I know of," Bud answered. "But it sure seems odd that someone would go to all the trouble of making a piece of gutter look like a murder weapon and putting it in Dusty's car. Dusty's saying she was setup, and it does look that way. I can't think of any other explanation."

"Well," Mason replied, "If so, it's a setup by someone who lives in the Dark Ages and has no idea we can test for fingerprints and blood types."

"Someone out of touch, like a groundskeeper in a remote mountain town who maybe drinks too much?" Bud asked.

"Could be, but surely Juno isn't that out of touch."

"Well, something else to think about in this convoluted case," Bud said. "Do you ever get the feeling things are never going to go anywhere? Are the CBI guys having any better luck than I am?"

"I don't know, Bud. If they are, they're sure not sharing anything with my office, which they normally would. That makes me think they're about as clueless as we are. Any new word on where Juno might be?"

"You'll know the minute I hear anything," Bud answered, then paused and added, "Wait, actually, I did hear some news and was going to call Deputy Chuck, but it slipped my mind. Too much going on. Someone said Juno was up in Marble hanging out with the woman who lives in an ice-cream wagon."

"I'll give Schofield a call and have him check it out. Thanks. Keep me posted if you hear anything else."

"Sure, you bet," Bud replied, hanging up, feeling that old familiar sense of frustration he'd felt from day one on this case and almost wishing he'd never heard of Redstone, the Ruby of the Rockies.

## 38

Bud had taken a break and bought a cup of coffee from the inn's restaurant and was now back in the big leather chair, laptop open. He still hadn't researched what he'd come here for, namely, ghosts.

He resisted the urge to check the weather, the Radium online newspaper, *The Radium Ray*, and the ads for used Airstream trailers. Instead, he cut right to the chase, entering the words "ghost skeptic" into the search bar. He knew if he just entered the word "ghost" he'd be sitting there for weeks reading about different ghost sightings and what they meant.

Surprisingly, Bud's first search result had the word "infrasound" in it. He clicked on the link and found a report titled, "UK Researchers Conduct Infrasound Experiment." Bud wasn't sure what infrasound was, so he read on:

*On May 31, 2003, a team of UK researchers exposed 700 people to music accompanied by infrasound waves. Infrasound is sound lower in frequency than 20 Hertz, the normal limit of human hearing. The experimental concert consisted of four musical pieces, two with the infrasound and two without. The participants were not told which pieces included the infrasound.*

*The presence of the tone resulted in a significant number (22%) of respondents reporting anxiety, uneasiness, extreme sorrow, nervous feelings of revulsion or fear, chills down the spine, and feelings of pressure on the chest.*

*In presenting the evidence to the British Association for the Advancement of Science, Professor Richard Wiseman said, "These results suggest that low frequency sound can cause people to have unusual experiences even though they cannot consciously detect infrasound. Some scientists have suggested that this level of sound may be present at some allegedly haunted sites and so cause people to have odd sensations that they attribute to a ghost—our findings support these ideas."*

Bud let out a low whistle. A scientific explanation for ghosts! He thought back to the evening he and the dogs had seen the ghost down by the river behind the Ice House Cafe, then went to the next link:

*Infrasound May be the Cause of Many Ghost Sightings*

*Computer specialist Vick Tandy from Coventry University had always been skeptical about ghost sightings until he had his own strange experience one late evening in the lab where he conducted experiments: he broke into a sweat, feeling that someone sinister was watching him. Soon, he saw a strange gray form cross the room and approach him, then disappear without a trace.*

*Tandy, being a scientist as well as amateur fencer, eventually was able to trace the cause of the weird apparition, thanks to an accidental event that occurred with his fencing rapier. He had brought the rapier into his lab to fine tune it for an event, and the blade began vibrating while he had it in a vise, as if some invisible hand was moving it.*

*Tandy soon discovered that the oscillations were being caused by very low sound waves, so low he was unable to hear them, waves coming from the air conditioner. The same waves had caused his eyes to also oscillate, creating the strange feeling and optical illusion earlier. He measured the waves at 18.98 hertz, the exact frequency that causes the human eye to resonate.*

Now Bud was caught up in reading about infrasound, and didn't notice he'd been sitting in the same position for over two hours, his leg going to sleep.

*If the theory is correct, infrasound is to blame for most ghost sightings, as well as the mystery of the various flying Dutchmen ships that wander the seas without crews. This includes the ship Maria Celesta, which, when boarded by seamen, was found to have a hot dinner recently served and still on the table, but nary a soul on board. Research shows that ocean waves under some conditions will resonate at 7 Hertz, which is devastating to people and will make them jump overboard to flee.*

Another site read:

*Sound waves of low frequency may appear quite often under natural conditions. Trains create infrasound, as do large bells and gongs. Strong gusts of wind hitting chimneys or towers create infrasound, and the low frequencies can penetrate through very thick walls. Tunnel-shaped corridors may further magnify the sounds, thus the reason why people often come across ghosts in long corridors of ancient castles. Such places are perfect for creating and amplifying infrasound.*

Bud was now sure that there had to be something in the Redstone Castle conducive to infrasound and thereby creating the illusion of the ghost of the Lion of Redstone, John Osgood, the very same ghost that had caused Callie distress.

Bud put down his computer, coming out of his semi-trance and shaking his leg. He pulled out his cell phone, dialing Dusty's number.

"Dusty, this is Bud. Do you have a minute for a few questions?" he asked when Dusty answered.

"Sure," she replied, "Though I can't take long. We're smack dab in the middle of getting ready for the big party."

Bud paused, then asked, "Say, would it be considered improper to ask if a couple of close friends could come along? We have guests, and I'd hate to leave them home alone."

"Of course they can come," Dusty said congenially. "I've had a couple of cancellations, so it's not a problem."

"Thanks a million. I think you'll enjoy meeting them. But as for my questions, and I'll try to make this brief, do you believe in ghosts?"

Bud could tell from the long pause that Dusty hadn't been prepared for his question. Finally, she answered, "I don't know, Bud. Maybe, but I'm just not sure."

"Well," he replied, "I can tell from your answer that you've never seen one. Is that correct? Not even since you moved into the castle?"

"That's correct, Bud. But Callie told me she'd seen one several times."

"Do you know where?"

"It was in her wing, I know that, because she was going to move into another wing, but she never had the chance."

"Dusty, bear with me, as I have a theory. Is there any kind of mechanical room in her wing?"

"Yes, that's where all the HVAC stuff is for the entire castle, back in a room behind her kitchen there."

Bud felt a sense of satisfaction—he may have just solved the sightings of the supposed ghost of John Osgood.

He continued, "OK, thanks. By the way, Sheriff Mason has given me permission to go into Callie's wing and look around. I just want to give you a head's up. I'll probably come check it out sometime tomorrow, if that works for you. Can I get into the castle, or will you be gone?"

There was a long pause, then Dusty finally said, "Bud, I don't feel comfortable with that at all. Let's talk about it later at the party."

"Why not?"

"You're not a lawman and, as a non-professional, I'm worried you might do something to hinder the investigation—unknowingly, of course. I'm sorry. We'll talk more later. Maybe if Deputy Schofield or someone goes in there with you we could work it out."

Bud felt like he'd been slapped, but managed to say a cordial goodbye anyway. He knew it was Dusty's way of getting back at him for refusing to work for her, and he could partly understand that, but he never thought she would actually hinder his investigation.

He stood, picking up his laptop, then left the inn and headed back down the boulevard to the cottage, forgetting he was carrying the restaurant's coffee cup, a cup with the words in red lettering, "The Ruby of the Rockies."

Bud figured he'd solved the mystery of Osgood's ghost, but he still had one more spirit to exorcise—the ghost he'd seen behind the Ice House Cafe.

## 39

Bud was glad to be back at the cottage, even though the gang hadn't yet returned from their drive to see the fall colors. The place seemed strangely quiet with everyone gone, and Bud wished they'd all get back soon.

He went out onto the veranda and watched as a few tourists wandered to the back of the Ice House Cafe to check out the giant marble icicle. A couple of kids tried to climb it, to no avail, slipping back down the slick marble onto the grass.

Bud sat once again in the big wicker chair, watching the sun go down over the canyon rim, thinking of how early the sun was setting. Part of it was the time of year, but part was because the little town was blocked in by canyon walls, which made the sun set at least a couple of hours earlier than it would out in the Big Empty by Green River.

He was tired, but he knew if he took a nap now, he would be up half the night, wide awake, so he sat up straight, not wanting to get too comfortable.

As he sat there, he thought he heard the click of the front door opening—it sounded like Doc and Millie and Wilma Jean might be back. He waited for the sound of their voices, as well as the pitter patter of little dog feet coming to see where he was, as the dogs always ran back to the veranda if he wasn't in the front room, looking for him. But all was quiet.

He was about to get up and go see what was going on when he felt a hand on his shoulder, making him nearly jump out of his skin.

"Howdy, Sheriff," Howie said. "I sure didn't mean to scare you, but Wilma Jean said to come on in, that you'd probably be back here."

Bud jumped up from the chair, almost tipping it over.

"Howie! You guys got here a day early. I thought you were coming tomorrow."

Howie sat down on the nearby wicker settee, his lanky frame taking up the entire seat, still dressed in his sheriff's uniform—tan khaki pants and shirt with emblems on the shoulders that read "Emery County, Utah."

"We were so excited we decided to come early. It's not every day you get to stay in a castle, you know," Howie replied, grinning. "We already took our stuff out there and met Dusty. I called your wife, and she said they'll be back soon. Maureen and Barry are getting coffee at the cafe next door."

"I'm glad you're here, Howie. We can all have dinner together at the Redstone Inn," Bud said.

Howie leaned back. "Man, I'm so tired I feel like I'm sleepwalking. That gal at the castle, Dusty, she's, well, a bit out of my league, Bud, kind of a critical person. Are you sure it's OK for us to stay there?"

"Sure, Howie. Why not? It's part of the deal."

"Well," Howie paused, then continued, "She reminds me of a story I heard when I went over to this training session over in Castle Dale, the one the mayor said I had to go to."

Howie continued. "This guy there, a policeman from Las Vegas, told the story about this time he was serving as security for a big to-do with some famous politician, and this woman pulled up in a Mercedes and wanted to park it there in the security zone. He told her no go, and she said, 'Officer, don't you know who I am?' Well, he looked at her and said, 'No, don't you?' She then said, 'Well, of course I know who I am,' and he said, 'Then why are you asking me?'"

"Pretty funny, Howie," Bud said, though he didn't really think it was very funny at all. He usually found Howie pretty entertaining—when he wasn't being frustrating, anyway. Oh well, Howie had said he was tired.

"Hey, Bud, what's that music I hear playing outside?"

Howie stood and looked out the veranda windows down the street, then said, "It's an ice-cream wagon! Let's go get a cone."

Bud suddenly had a strange sense come over him, a sense that something was a bit off. He hesitated. Why would an ice-cream truck be in Redstone? It then occurred to him that it might be the woman from Marble, and maybe Juno was with her. Bud jumped to his feet, following Howie out the door.

It was indeed an ice-cream truck, and the woman driver stopped upon seeing Bud and Howie, asking them what they wanted. Howie ordered a strawberry cone, and Bud asked for vanilla, but the driver told them she was out of both flavors.

"Jump in, and we'll run over to my storehouse and get more," she offered. It was then that Bud realized the driver had to indeed be Barb Somerset, the woman from Marble. It seemed odd that she was now selling ice cream and needed to restock at her storehouse, but when she added that she needed help loading her ice-cream freezers, Bud and Howie jumped in.

"Say," Bud asked. "Have you seen Juno?" He was hoping that maybe Barb would tell him where Juno was hiding.

"No, I've never been to Alaska, though I've always wanted to go," Barb answered.

"No, I mean Juno Alaska," Bud replied, puzzled. Surely she knew he was referring to a person—after all, she supposedly knew Juno well.

"Yes, that's what I thought you meant," she said, giving him an odd look. "I've never been there."

Bud had a very surreal feeling—it seemed he was in a sort of alternate reality, yet everything looked the same as usual. He pinched himself to see if he was dreaming, but he felt it, so he decided he must be awake.

He'd had strange dreams before, when his subconscious seemingly got tired of his bumbling around and forced him to analyze things he was ignoring, whether intentional or not, but this seemed real.

Now the truck was whizzing along, and they soon were climbing a steep narrow road up the side of a mountain.

"Where exactly is your freezer?" Bud asked a bit nervously. Barb seemed to be going way too fast for the conditions, and the truck rocked back and forth with the ruts in the narrow road.

"I lease a small section of the Yule Marble Quarry," Barb answered. "It's underground, so everything stays colder. It's in the old section where they're no longer mining. We're almost there."

Barb pulled up next to a large gaping hole in the side of the mountain. They all got out and walked into the huge cavern, its walls glowing an eerie gray-white from the marble walls. Huge chunks the size of dump-truck beds sat near the opening in the dim evening light, waiting to be hauled away. It appeared to Bud that the quarry had shut down for the day, as there was no one there, even though there was equipment everywhere.

Howie looked around, slowly turning in a circle. "Amazing," he said with awe.

"So," Bud said, "This is where they got the marble for the Tomb of the Unknowns, also called the Tomb of the Unknown Soldier."

Barb looked irritated. "We need to get the ice cream and get out of here," she said. "This place gives me the creeps."

Just then, Bud saw a shadowy figure walk out onto a platform high above them, an area where the crews were using big drills to cut huge chunks of marble from the pure white walls.

"Hello, Mr. Shumway."

It was Juno! Bud was surprised, but managed to say hello in reply.

So, he thought, this was where Juno was hiding out. No wonder no one could find him.

"Are you working here now, Juno?" Bud asked.

"The sheriff is looking for me, isn't he?" Juno replied, ignoring Bud's question.

"Yes," Bud answered. "If you didn't do it, why not give up the chase and get the questioning over with?"

"Do what?" asked Barb.

"I'm here to tell you something important, Mr. Shumway," Juno replied.

"Go ahead," Bud said.

"Hannah doesn't need to worry about ever seeing that ghost she's afraid of. Tell her that for me, would you?"

"I hope you're right, but how would you know?" Bud replied, a bit mystified.

"Just a hunch," said Juno. "Actually, not a hunch, a fact. Oh, and you might consider that bass fishing really isn't an innocent sport like it might seem. Someone always gets hurt, even if it's just the fish. But I have to go now."

Juno was suddenly gone, and Bud wondered how someone could disappear so quickly. Must be some trick with the shadows, he figured. But why would Juno come all the way to the quarry to tell Bud that Hannah didn't need to worry? It didn't make sense.

Just then, Bud felt something cold in his hand. He looked down to see he was holding an ice-cream cone, and it was quickly melting, dripping down his arm. He dropped it to the ground, but now it felt like he had ice cream all over his face.

Bud suddenly woke, Hoppie licking his face and Pierre licking his hand and arm, too short to reach his face.

It had all been a dream.

Bud rubbed his eyes, trying to wake up. He tried to shrug the feeling of strangeness off, then reached down and picked Hoppie up, dragging him up onto his lap, then likewise with Pierre. The dogs felt comforting and familiar, and he was glad they were here.

Bud shook his head, thinking it might be a good idea to stay off the ice cream for awhile. He could now hear Wilma Jean laughing in the other room.

He couldn't remember ever being so glad to hear her voice.

# 40

Bud and Doc Richardson sat on the banks of the Crystal River, watching as golden leaves from the nearby cottonwoods floated gently down into the water and then on by.

The trees would soon be bare at this rate, thought Bud, and the valley would definitely soon wear the cloak of winter. He was glad he and Wilma Jean would be over in Radium by then, where the climate was a bit warmer.

Doc was holding a long branch he'd broken from a nearby willow, letting the end trail in the shallow waters near the bank, occasionally catching a leaf or two. The dogs were asleep under a nearby tree, stretched out in the tall grass.

"I just can't figure this case out," Bud said with frustration. "We're about ready to head out, and I'm thinking I'll never get any closure here. I'll have to leave it up to the Pitkin County Sheriff's Office and the CBI to solve Callie's murder, I guess. But I hate to concede defeat."

Bud normally had no one to talk to about such things, even though Wilma Jean was happy to listen when she wasn't too busy and had given him many helpful tips in the past. Having Doc Richardson here was a real treat, as the Doc had seen it all when he'd been coroner, and his keen analytic mind knew exactly where to look for obtuse clues. He'd helped Bud before, and Bud was hoping he could shed some light on things again for him.

"The big party's tonight, huh?" Doc said, seeming to ignore what Bud had just said.

"Tonight. I hope Howie and the crew get here soon. They'll need time to set up, plus he's supposed to have my dress jacket. No way I'm going to rent another suit."

"That reminds me, there was a jacket on the chair on the front porch this morning when I got up. I put it on the chair in the kitchen."

"I saw that," Bud replied. "It's the one I put in Juno's car when I thought he might get stuck out in bad weather. It means he's maybe back around, as he was probably the one who returned it. I actually thought I'd never see it again."

"Well, it shows he has a certain level of integrity, to return it," Doc said. "But as for your dream, there have to be some important clues there, if you can only figure out what they are, Bud. We've talked about these dreams you have before, and to me it seems like you have them when your brain has an amalgamation of clues, enough to solve the crime, but your conscious mind just isn't processing them yet. Seems like your subconscious is a bit ahead of things and is trying to tell you to get with the program."

"I agree," Bud replied. "It does feel that way. But I'm pretty much stymied this time, Doc. Nothing in the dream makes sense. Why would I dream that Juno would tell me to give Hannah a message like that?"

"You know as well as I do that things aren't always what they seem, especially in dreams. Is it possible that the emotions you felt in the dream carry more clues than the words?"

"Well, I pretty much felt like everything was totally off through the entire dream, Doc, so I don't think so."

"Maybe the dream was trying to get you to step out of the world you operate in and into an unreal world. Maybe it was telling you the murderer doesn't operate in the same emotional plane that you and I do."

"How am I supposed to do something like that—step into the mind of someone who lives in a fantasy world?"

"I don't know, Bud. I'm just coming up with suggestions. Talking about things can trigger thoughts that might be helpful, take you in new directions."

"The dream didn't seem to have anything much going on in it, did it?" continued Doc. "That's why I'm thinking maybe the message wasn't one of action as much as one of feeling and analysis."

"Being in the ice-cream truck was very surreal," Bud said thoughtfully. "But not nearly as strange as the marble quarry. And Juno showing up to give me a strange message for Hannah..."

"A message that she needn't worry about ever seeing the ghost. That seems strange to me also, Bud, yet if you could decipher it, it feels like it might be the clue you need to proceed with all this."

"Agreed, and yet my mind is saying there was something else in the dream that I'm overlooking, something that was an even bigger clue."

"Did the joke that Howie told about the cop doing security trigger anything?"

"No, that seemed to just be a distraction. But maybe it was my mind telling me that the Howie in my dream was an imposter. Howie doesn't have to rely on jokes or dumb stories to be funny, he's just naturally a bit goofy."

Doc smiled. "Agreed. He's one of a kind. But why would you dream about an imposter? Is it possible that Howie represented someone else? That what he was saying or doing wasn't to be interpreted literally, but maybe more as a type of road sign? A way for your subconscious to tell you that you're not seeing someone in the right way? Your mind could very well be trying to get you to see someone in a new light, so it cloaks that person in a different persona."

"I just don't know, Doc. I've never been good at this kind of thing, you know that. That's why I'm asking you. I've never put much stock in dream analysis. I mostly think it's just your brain running amok while the rest of your body's asleep and not governing things."

"Well, the kind of analysis where certain things are symbolic of the same thing for everyone, I myself don't believe that's true. Like where someone dreams about the color red and it always means they're angry, that sort of thing. I think our dreams are tailored to our own experiences."

"I pretty much agree there, Doc. So, who would Howie have really been in my dream?"

"I don't know. What did he make you feel like?"

Bud was silent for some time, thinking, trying to remember the dream in detail. Finally, he said, "Hannah. He evoked that same feeling that she does in me. Kind of a lack of boundaries, like when Howie just walked in and put his hand on my shoulder. That's something I could see her doing. And the real Howie's very tolerant, and this Howie wasn't, like when he criticized Dusty. Hannah's kind of gossipy and likes to know everything that's going on."

Bud could now hear Wilma Jean's voice, and he knew Howie and the band had arrived. The dogs sat up, ears perked forward, then took off trotting to the cottage.

"Think of what Howie said in the dream, and maybe it was really a clue about Hannah," Doc advised. "But it looks like we have company."

He stood, letting the stick float on down the river.

Bud followed him up the hill to the cottage, lost in thought, not even noticing the figure watching them from the upstairs window of the Ice House Cafe.

# 41

It was indeed Howie and Maureen, their little green VW bug stuffed to the gills with musical equipment and their sound system. Chaos engulfed the formerly quiet cottage as everyone said hello and got caught up. It had been some time since Howie and Maureen had seen Doc and Millie.

Before long, Wilma Jean and Millie had taken off in Millie and Doc's car, leading the way to the castle, followed by Howie and Maureen. Wilma Jean was now in her element—she would introduce them to Dusty and make sure everything went smoothly with the accommodations and setup for the night's party.

Barry, their bass player, was also on his way, but an hour behind them, as he'd had to wait to get off work at the highway department.

Now Doc decided it would be a good time to mosey down the boulevard to a particular art gallery where Millie had admired a marble sculpture she'd wanted for their garden back in Palisade. He would give it to her as a surprise when they got home.

Bud sat down in the big wicker chair in the veranda and thought for a few minutes, then pulled out his phone and dialed the Pitkin County Courthouse.

"Sheriff Mason here."

"It's Bud Shumway, Sheriff. I need to ask you a few questions, if you have time."

"Sure, go ahead, Bud."

"It's about the 911 call from Juno. Did you personally listen to it?"

"I did, why?"

"It was muffled, right?"

"It was."

"Are you 100 percent sure that Juno said he'd seen blood on the forehead?"

"I'm sure, why?"

"Did anyone else listen to it?"

"Where's this going, Bud? Of course I had others listen to it. My detectives did, as well as the CBI."

"Look, Sheriff, could you do me a favor, I mean a really big one? I think I know who killed Callie, and I need to have that call analyzed by someone who can run it through a computer and do voice recognition on it, someone who does this professionally."

Mason paused, then sounded a bit uncomfortable. "I guess I can do that, though I don't see the point."

"I need it now," Bud replied. "I'm leaving town day after tomorrow, Sheriff, and without it, I can't do anything."

"Do you mind telling me what this is about?" Mason asked. "I already had a number of professionals listen to that tape, Bud. Voice recognition software's just going to verify what we heard. If you're trying to get Juno off the hook, it's not going to work."

"Look," Bud replied a bit testily. "I thought we were on the same page here—to try and figure out who killed Callie. I'm absolutely sure it wasn't Juno, and that tape will vindicate him. I don't think he said what everyone thinks he said."

Mason sighed. "Alright. I can email the digital version to the guy over in Denver who does this. I'll call him and see if he'll do a rush job. I'll call you back. I'm anxious to know what you're thinking."

"Thanks, and there's something else..."

"Oh?"

"I want to get into Callie's suite today. Dusty's already told me I can't go in there, even though I told her I had your permission."

"Why would she do that?"

"I have my theories. But I'm wondering if I were to let myself in if it would be considered trespassing."

"Not as far as I'm concerned. I could send a deputy down to let you in, if you want, but we're shorthanded and it won't be today."

"Are you coming to the party tonight?"

"No, I wasn't planning on it. I'm just not ready to see all of Callie's friends, Bud. It's still too raw for me, as well as the idea of being in her house. Too many memories. Look, Dusty doesn't own the castle yet, it's still in probate. Technically, she can't legally tell anyone what to do there, so if you go into Callie's wing, you're not breaking any laws as far as I'm concerned, and no one in my office would arrest you. Getting in may be another matter, as she has the only key, except the one we have."

"OK, thanks. I'll figure something out."

"Keep me posted, Bud, and I'll call you as soon as I get this voice recognition thing back, assuming he can do it ASAP. It would sure mean a lot to me to see this case closed and Callie's murderer brought to justice."

"Me too," Bud replied thoughtfully. "I'll let you know what I find out. And thanks, I think I'm on to something, I really do."

"Maybe," Mason replied. "But I want to tell you I bought some of those beads you were talking about, you know, to help me think. So far, they work great. Thanks for the tip."

Bud hung up, smiling.

His smile didn't last long, though, and he knew he felt less certain than he'd sounded on the phone. He had a hunch, but if he were wrong, he was back to square zero on who Callie's murderer was.

For some reason, he felt it just couldn't be Juno, yet he had nothing to substantiate that claim. Mason's certainty about Juno saying he'd seen blood on Callie's forehead made Bud feel even less confident, especially if the CBI guys agreed with that analysis.

After all, the CBI were the experts—much more so than he was, that was for sure, with their extensive training, equipment, and experience. What right did he, basically an untrained ex-lawman from a tiny desert town in Utah, have to question the experts?

But he also knew that the recording could mean life in prison for Juno, and he felt something was wrong.

Now Bud leaned back and thought of all the things Doc had said about his dream. He just couldn't get Juno's statement out of his mind, the one that Hannah didn't need to worry about ever seeing the ghost.

Bud pulled the little notebook from his shirt pocket and opened it to where he'd written what Hannah had yelled from her window that strange morning. As he read, he began fingering the beads around his neck.

*There's blood everywhere, Mr. Shumway. Blood on the forehead. Blood on the headboard. Blood on the moon and blood on the Unknown's Tomb. The zombie will pay, she'll pay with her life.*

Blood on the headboard? How had he missed that? He had only heard forehead. Had Juno actually said headboard and the 911 operator had also heard forehead? And why did Hannah say both headboard and forehead?

Suddenly, Bud sat bolt upright. If it had been a snake it would've bit him, he thought. It seemed all too obvious—if Hannah *were* the ghost, she would never have to worry about seeing it.

But how could Hannah be a ghost? And hadn't he decided the ghost was, as they say, *in the machine*, the result of infrasound?

Maybe John Osgood's ghost was the result of infrasound, Bud thought, but hadn't Callie written in her diary about also seeing a female ghost?

Bud jumped up, slipped his Ruger into its shoulder holster, gave the dogs each a couple of Barkie Biscuits, and headed out in Wilma Jean's big Lincoln to the Redstone Castle.

## 42

"Sheriff, I have a question for you," Howie said to Bud, his arms all tangled in electrical cords.

They were in the castle's large dance hall, setting up sound equipment for the evening party.

"Shoot away," Bud replied.

"Well, I've always wondered, you know, they talk about private investigators and then shorten it to 'P.I.,' then some people say 'private eye.' Well, is that 'private eye' as in someone who sees and looks for clues with their eye, or is it 'private I' as in 'I' for 'Investigator'?"

Bud groaned. "I don't know, Howie. In fact, I'm now totally confused."

"Sorry," Howie said apologetically.

"It's OK," Bud replied. "But Howie, I have to go in a minute. I have some business in another part of the castle. But I have a question for you. Did the mayor ever send you over to some kind of training session in Castle Dale, where you met an officer from Las Vegas?"

"Not that I recall, Sheriff. Did you meet someone who said they'd met me there or something?"

"No, Howie. It's not important. I'll tell you about it sometime when the smoke clears. I'll be back shortly. Carry on."

With that, Bud looked around to see if Dusty were nearby, and, seeing no one, headed for Callie's wing. He knew it was locked, but he had a plan that he hoped would work.

When Bud was young, growing up in the center of Utah's Uranium Boom, he'd become interested in the history of the Cold War. He'd later become a uranium miner, but an unsettling near-fatal accident had resulted in him changing careers, and he'd become a lawman instead.

But before all that happened, while researching the Cold War, he'd learned about Richard Feynman, the lead physicist of the Manhattan Project in Las Alamos, where the atomic bomb had been invented. But what interested Bud most about Feynman wasn't his Nobel Prize winning brilliance in physics, but rather Feynman's ability to pick locks.

Bud had gone through a period when he'd tried to emulate Feynman, developing various lock-picking techniques, but he'd eventually lost interest at about the same time he entered high school and figured out that girls were more interested in guys who *owned* hot cars than in guys who could *steal* hot cars, not that he ever took it that far.

Now, as Bud stealthily slipped through the castle to Callie's wing, he hoped his lock-picking abilities would come back to him, even though he hadn't used them since he was a kid.

He was soon at a large wooden door with police tape stuck all over it next to a sign that read, "Do Not Enter Under Sheriff's Orders —Violators Will Be Arrested."

Bud quickly pulled out a credit card and began working the lock. He slid the card between the door jamb and the door, then tilted the card so it almost touched the door knob. He hoped it wasn't a dead-bolt—if so, his technique wouldn't work.

The card now slipped under the bolt, forcing it into the door, and while Bud leaned against the door, it popped open, creaking a little as it swung on its hinges. Bud nearly fell down. He quickly recovered and went inside, closing the door behind him and locking it.

As he put the card back into his wallet, he noticed it was now hopelessly bent. He hoped Wilma Jean had hers so they could get home, as it didn't look like his was going to be of any further use.

Bud now stood for a moment, shocked at how easily he'd entered Callie's wing.

This wing of the castle was more like an apartment and modern looking, unlike the rest of the castle, which still had a period feel to it. Callie's quarters were bright and airy feeling, with paintings on the walls of Western scenes—primarily horses and hayfields and meadows with cattle grazing. One wall was covered with various recording awards the singer had received, including numerous gold and platinum records.

After Bud looked around a bit and got his bearings, he wasn't really sure where to start. He decided the bedroom would be the best place, since it had been the scene of Callie's murder.

He hesitantly entered the room, overcome for a moment by a deep sense of sadness, the murder seeming more real, now that he was where Callie had died. It all seemed so unnecessary, the tragic ending of a life that had contributed so much to so many, both financially and through musical enjoyment.

Callie's bedroom was well lit, sunlight streaming in through a large window that framed the stunning redrock cliffs above the castle. The room was furnished with a large antique sleigh bed, and Bud wondered if it weren't the very same one that Osgood and his wife had slept in. He noted the blankets and sheets were still disheveled, just like they'd been when Callie had been killed.

Bud was now reluctant to continue. This was the part of his job that he hated most, the sorting through the evidence part, and he wasn't even getting paid to do it this time.

He wondered yet again what was motivating him to continue. He'd said it was because he wanted justice for Callie, but he'd never even met her. Perhaps it was because she looked so much like his wife, Wilma Jean, and he'd become somewhat unable to divorce himself from her case emotionally.

Now he noticed that a large pool of dried blood darkened the pearl-colored sheets, and he felt a pang of anxiety, as if he would soon see the actual victim, even though he knew Callie's body had long been removed from the scene.

His gaze now turned upwards, to the massive headboard, and what he saw gave him pause—there, in the exact center, was a handprint of dried blood, perfectly preserved. Had the CBI and Mason's detectives seen it and taken fingerprints? Surely they had.

And now Bud knew Juno had to be innocent. If he'd come into the room, he surely would have seen the blood. He had to have called 911 saying he'd seen blood on the headboard, not on the forehead. It was very possible he hadn't even seen Callie's body, as by then it was probably lying off the deck in the dark.

Bud had seen all he needed to see. He knew the CBI had scoured the room for clues, and there was nothing he could add to that.

He turned to go when his toe caught on something up under the bottom of the bed frame. He bent to see what it was.

It was dark under there, and yet he could see there was something bright yellow with tiny black spots. Something on the end of the object was caught on the toe of his boot, and he carefully pulled his boot back, the object coming with it.

He could now see it clearly. It was a jitterbug fishing lure, resembling a chubby little fish, the same kind Gene had worn on his suit lapel at Callie's memorial service.

Bud now recalled Juno's words in his dream: *You might consider that bass fishing really isn't an innocent sport like it might seem. Someone always gets hurt, even if it's just the fish.*

Now it struck him—this was an important clue he'd been overlooking, a clue that maybe Gene wasn't as innocent as he seemed. It hadn't made sense at the time, but his subconscious was now reading it very clearly. He just hadn't considered Gene to be much of a suspect, and he obviously needed to rethink that lapse in his detective work, now that he'd found the jitterbug.

Bud now very carefully took a plastic baggie from his jacket pocket and picked up the lure, careful not to touch it. It was then he noticed several strands of hair caught in the hook—blonde hair the exact same color as Calico Callie's.

Bud put the baggie into his jacket pocket and slipped out the patio door. He soon noticed what looked like fresh tracks in the garden, tracks that had the word "Goodyear" embossed in them. He wondered what Juno was doing back on the castle grounds, but he didn't have time to stop and analyze them.

He was soon back to Wilma Jean's big pink Lincoln Continental and on his way back to the cottage, where a phone call would ensure that Deputy Chuck Schofield would meet him to collect the fishing lure, what Bud hoped would be new piece of evidence.

## 43

Howie sat backwards in a folding chair, his long legs stretched out and his arms hanging over the chair's back as he eyed the sound equipment now displayed on the castle's stage.

"Well, we're all set up and ready to go, Sheriff," he said to Bud, who had returned to the castle after meeting Chuck and handing off the fishing lure. "Now what?"

"It's almost lunch time, Howie. Let's go get a sandwich at the cafe."

"OK, but I brought my metal detector. Maybe we should go out to one of the mine dumps and check it out."

Bud now recalled what Gus had told him earlier about Juno burying things.

"You know, Howie, all the mine dumps are up in the high country. I don't think we're going to have time to drive up there, given the day's half over and we need to be back for the party. But we could check out that meadow over there."

"I'll go get my detector out of the car. Where'd the gals go, anyway?"

"They wanted to show Maureen some of the little shops on the boulevard. We're supposed to meet them at the cottage later," Bud replied. "Doc, too."

Bud noted that Gene's BMW was now back, parked in front of the castle. He paused, thinking, then said, "I need to make a quick call, Howie. I'll meet you out back."

As Howie went to get his brand new Bounty Hunter Quick Draw metal detector, Bud dialed Deputy Schofield's number. He thought again of how Sprocket's dogs had gone to the car and wondered if it might not be prudent to search it.

After a brief conversation, Deputy Chuck said he would call and see if he could get a search warrant, though he knew the CBI would be the ones to actually conduct the search, and it probably wouldn't be happening today.

Howie was soon beside Bud with the metal detector and a small shovel, and the pair began walking through the big meadow that flanked the castle, stretching to Gus Dearhammer's cabin some ways off.

As they walked along, Bud noticed more sandal tracks, all with the word "Goodyear," and he knew Juno had also come this way, and from the looks of the tracks, quite recently.

Had he come to dig up whatever he'd buried? Bud decided they should keep an eye out, for if Juno had buried something of importance here, he might not be very cordial about demanding its return if they should find it.

They walked along, eyes to the ground, Bud occasionally scanning the trees lining the meadow for any sign of Juno.

Suddenly, Howie stopped, pointing to the ground.

"Look Sheriff. This could be a good spot. Someone buried something here—either that, or there's ground squirrels around."

He turned on his metal detector and held it above a spot where the ground was disturbed, looking indeed like someone had buried something.

"Bingo!" Howie said excitedly. "There's something there, alright. The detector's going nuts!"

Bud was now carefully digging, wondering what they would find. He hoped it wasn't something he would prefer to not find.

But before he knew it, he and Howie were looking at the business end of a shotgun—a shotgun held by none other than Juno Alaska. Bud appreciated how accurate his intuition had been concerning Juno being in the area, but he didn't think much of his own ability to stand guard.

Juno said, "Dig it up real slow, Mr. Shumway. I don't want to shoot this thing, but believe me, I will."

There was a resolve in his voice that told Bud he would indeed shoot if he saw the need.

Bud began digging again, and soon saw part of a plastic bag sticking out of the ground. Howie stood by, looking grim and unsure of what was going on and even less sure of what to do about it.

Bud carefully pulled the bag from the ground. It contained what looked like a rock hammer.

Bud asked, "What is it?"

Juno replied, "It's the murder weapon—what was used to kill Callie."

"The murder weapon? How do you know that?"

"I can't tell you."

"Did you use it to kill Callie, Juno? If so, your prints are all over it."

"I didn't kill Callie. Now put it down in the dirt and step back away."

Bud placed the bag with the hammer in it on the ground as he was told, then stepped away. Howie followed behind him, not wanting to be any closer to Juno's shotgun than necessary.

Juno now walked over and picked up the bag, holding the shotgun on Bud and Howie the whole time. He then carefully stuck it into his jacket pocket.

"If you didn't kill Callie, then how did you know where the weapon was buried?" Bud asked.

"I knew because I buried it," Juno replied.

"So, you know who killed Callie?"

"I do."

"You realize that protecting a criminal is a crime?" Bud asked.

"I know that, but I ain't protecting no criminal."

"Whoever killed Callie is a criminal, Juno."

"Not this time."

"What?" Bud asked incredulously.

"They're innocent," Juno stated.

"How can you murder someone and be innocent?"

"It can happen," Juno said solemnly. "It did happen."

Bud shook his head. "It just doesn't make sense. You can't murder someone and be innocent, Juno, you just can't."

"You can, Mr. Shumway."

"Was it an accident?" Bud asked.

"I don't know if a judge would call it that or not. Probably not."

"What are you going to do with the hammer?"

Bud thought back to the coroner's report, and the small hammer matched perfectly to the murder weapon.

"I'm gonna throw it in the river."

"That's tampering with evidence, Juno. You'll end up in prison. Besides, there's that 911 call you made. That's possible evidence."

"You can't ever prove it was the murder weapon if you can't finger-print it. I told you it was, but I could be lying. I could be making this all up as some kind of game. It wouldn't hold up in court. And the same for that call. The sheriff may think I said something self-incriminating, but I didn't."

Bud knew Juno was right. The definitive analysis of the call would come soon, Bud hoped, but he hadn't thought it was much to go on in the first place.

And Bud knew Juno was right about the hammer not being any kind of evidence if it were missing. Bud hadn't even really got a chance to look at it. All he knew was that he had dug up a hammer in a plastic bag out in some meadow and handed it to Juno. Juno could never be convicted on that kind of flimsy evidence.

"Mason's just wanting to show his rich Aspen weasels he's doing something by arresting me," Juno added.

"I can't answer to that, Juno, but I can tell you that Mason's no longer on the case. But you do realize I can have you arrested for threatening me with a weapon?"

"Not any more."

Juno now held the shotgun down by his side and said, "I ain't threatening you and your friend, Mr. Shumway. Let's just let this thing go. You'll be real sorry if you don't. Go on back home and forget all this, enjoy your life back in Utah."

"It seems like you're still threatening us, Juno."

"No. When I say you'll be sorry, it's just that you'll realize I was right and be sorry you didn't let it go, because the person is innocent and who knows what will happen to...never mind. I ain't sayin' another word about this 'cause I might screw up and let on who it is."

"So, it's someone I know?"

"Not another word. You have a good day, Mr. Shumway, both you and your friend here. And next time you talk to the sheriff or whoever's on the case, you might consider telling them it was all a mistake. Justice can never be served here because it wasn't a case of being unjust—it's just what it is."

Bud began fiddling with the beads around his neck. He knew he could go for his Ruger, but it seemed like a bad idea and unnecessary.

Finally, Bud said, "Juno, if you give me the hammer, I'll send it to the lab. You picked it up from Callie's bedroom, right? And you were careful to not get your own fingerprints on it, correct?"

After some thought, Juno said, "I know you're trying to trick me. I'm not falling for it, Mr. Shumway."

"I have no evidence against the real murderer unless you give me the weapon, Juno. If you take it, they're going to get off scot free."

"You think I did it, don't you?" asked Juno.

"No, I'm sure you didn't. Do you want justice for Callie, Juno?"

"I do, but I don't want who killed her to be harmed, either. They're innocent."

"You can't have it both ways, Juno. You don't have the right to keep the rest of us from ever knowing what happened to Callie, and you can't play God."

Bud was surprised at how swiftly and unexpectedly Juno moved, tossing the bag with the hammer in it at Howie's feet.

Then, in mere seconds, Juno slipped into the trees and was gone.

## 44

Deputy Chuck Scofield was surprised to get yet another call from Bud, but he answered without sounding a bit surprised or irritated, though Bud suspected he was both.

"You have the possible murder weapon?" Chuck asked incredulously. "That's great news, Bud. I'll meet you at your house. I'm going to deliver this one personally to the sheriff. They sent a deputy down to get the fishing lure, but it was hard to find someone that could get free."

"What's going on up there now?" Bud asked.

"The Chair of the Federal Reserve was flying in for a conference when her plane skidded off the runway. No one was hurt, but they have deputies out there doing crowd control, or I should say, pepperazzi control. I swear, half of Aspen is the rich and famous, and the other half is the pepperazzi. The people who clean their houses and work in the stores and schools all live down valley. Aspen's gonna be in a world of hurt if there's ever a rockslide on Highway 82. I can't see Cher as a grocery-store checker."

Bud laughed. "Probably all too true, but don't you mean paparazzi? OK, I'll be back at the cottage in a few minutes. You can meet my friend and ex-colleague, Sheriff Howie McPherson from Green River. Are you going to the party?"

"I am," Chuck replied. "If I can get back in time. My wife's anxious to tour the castle. Might be her last chance. Rumor has it that Dusty's going to sell it."

"Well, that has to be just a rumor," Bud replied. "Because we don't even know yet if she's the one who will inherit it."

"Good point," Chuck said. "But I heard that Callie's attorney's going to be at the party and announce something important."

"No kidding?" Bud replied with surprise.

They said goodbye, and Bud slipped into the driver's seat of Wilma Jean's Lincoln and headed for the cottage. He would meet Deputy Schofield, then change clothes and go back to the castle, where the party was set to start in an hour.

Soon after meeting Chuck, Bud followed Wilma Jean, Doc and Millie, and Howie and Maureen and Barry in through the big front doors of the castle. A fellow dressed like a butler greeted them, taking their coats, though Bud opted to keep his tweed jacket, as it was a bit chilly, and Howie and the band obviously didn't want to part with their rhinestone-encrusted band jackets.

The large castle ballroom was already filled with people dressed to kill, all talking, most of them seeming to know each other. Bud felt self-conscious in his tweed jacket, which had served him well in Green River at various funerals, weddings, and such. He felt out of place among the Armani suits and long formal gowns that most of the guests were wearing.

It seemed contradictory to Bud that Callie Jensen, who had loved country music and the down-to-earth people it had sprung from, would have the opposite types of people at a dinner party in her memory. But Bud understood well the human need to impress one another. Even Wilma Jean and Millie were dressed like Bud had never seen them, wearing attire he'd seen only on the cover of women's fashion magazines, obviously the result of a recent shopping trip.

Bud was taken back by how much Wilma Jean resembled Callie, as was everyone else there, who kept giving her second glances, and he could tell a few were asking Dusty about her.

The room just kept filling up, and Bud wasn't sure he wouldn't get claustrophobic and have to leave, as he wasn't used to being around such large groups of people.

Now he noted a few people who weren't as well dressed—people like the waitress from the Redstone Inn and some of the shop keepers from the boulevard. A few looked like they'd made an effort to *not* be well dressed, and Bud recognized them as marble sculptors he'd seen in the various galleries. This made Bud feel less self-conscious and more able to relax and enjoy people watching.

As the evening wore on, it appeared that everyone had finally arrived, and the butler disappeared into the kitchen, where Bud figured he must be transforming himself into a waiter or such.

But the door opened one more time, and Bud was surprised to see Hannah enter. He half expected to see Juno trailing behind her, though he knew it would be suicide for him to show his face, since there was an arrest warrant out for him.

Hannah wore a very simple flowing dress with pockets that appeared to be made of some gauzy material. She also wore sandals and a tiara of fresh flowers that held back her long hair. She reminded Bud of someone from the old hippy days when flower power was big, even though it turned out eventually to be not all that big nor powerful.

The dress seemed familiar to Bud for some reason, though he couldn't quite place it. He then noticed that Hannah's left foot was wrapped in a large bandage and she was limping.

Dusty greeted everyone, walking around the crowd and telling everyone how happy Callie would have been to have them here. The result was probably the opposite of what she intended—instead of making the crowd happy, it left them subdued and pensive. One exception was the small crowd around Howie and the band, who seemed to be reveling in the band's glitzy Grand Ole Opry style costumes.

Howie's matching cowboy boots and Stetson with the embedded rhinestone flying saucers were a big hit, and if Bud recalled correctly, Maureen had given them to him for his birthday.

Dinner consisted of a catered gourmet feast with servers dressed in country-western suits and cowboy hats. By then, everyone seemed to have relaxed and were enjoying themselves. Bud guessed there were at least a hundred people there and wondered what it must have cost to cater a party like that.

Soon, Dusty introduced Callie's attorney, Robert Daniels, Esquire, who announced he would read a section of Callie's will over Alaska Flambé, which Bud found to be an interesting choice of dessert, given Dusty's dislike for Juno.

Bud thought reading the will over dessert was an unusual way to do things, but he figured Callie had wanted it done this way.

As Mr. Daniels began reading, everyone seemed surprised and pleased to hear the news. Callie had left a trust fund of over two million dollars for college scholarships for students from both Redstone and Marble, and in addition, she'd set up a fund to help the indigent of the area.

Everyone clapped, and the attorney smiled and sat down next to Dusty and Gene. When Dusty whispered to him, he nodded his head no, then pointed to something in the will. Dusty immediately turned red, got up, and left the room, followed by Gene.

Bud wondered who would receive the majority of Callie's estate, which he knew consisted of at the very least the castle and a good sum of money. Maybe it wasn't who Dusty thought it would be, Bud speculated.

Now Bud noted that Hannah had stood and walked to the buffet table, still limping. He watched her closely, wondering if she were going for seconds, but he stiffened when he saw her surreptitiously slip a large knife up the sleeve of her dress and then casually amble out the room in the direction of Callie's apartment.

Bud was irritated. He was enjoying the party more than he figured he would, and Howie and the Ramblin' Road Rangers were now set to take center stage. He didn't want to miss this, their first paying concert.

He had no idea what Hannah intended to do, but he knew he had to follow and find out.

## 45

Bud followed Hannah, staying back far enough that she wouldn't notice him. He was glad he'd checked out Callie's wing yesterday, as it gave him a familiarity with the castle that let him sneak around better.

Hannah was soon at the big door that led into Callie's apartment, and Bud wondered how she would deal with it being locked. Given how quickly she'd come back here, he knew she'd been here before.

Sure enough, she pulled a credit card from a pocket in her dress and quickly opened the door. Bud could tell she was well-practiced at it, and he barely managed to stick his toe in the door before it closed.

He waited a few minutes for her to proceed, then cautiously opened the door further and looked in. She was gone, so he slipped in, quickly ducking into the kitchen, wondering exactly where she was.

He didn't have to wonder long, as he soon heard her talking. She was back in Callie's bedroom, and Bud carefully slipped back into the hallway, staying just out of her view.

He could now hear Hannah clearly, even though what she was saying made no sense.

"The zombie will die. Everyone knows the zombie killed the beautiful Callie, and now the zombie must pay with her own life."

Bud was startled. The voice didn't really sound like Hannah, yet it did, though it was different somehow. He then realized it was the same voice he'd heard yelling at him from Hannah's window above the Ice House Cafe. It was Hannah, yet somehow not really Hannah.

Bud carefully peeked around the doorjamb into Callie's bedroom. There stood Hannah, looking at the blood on the headboard, visibly disturbed and shaking. Bud could see that Hannah had opened the patio door for some reason.

"The zombie must die. Is the zombie ready to die? It's been too long coming..."

Now Hannah pulled the knife from her sleeve and held it to her own throat.

Bud startled. Was Hannah going to kill herself? Suddenly, Juno's words in his dream came back to him:

*Hannah doesn't need to worry about ever seeing that ghost she's afraid of. Tell her that for me, would you?*

Bud now entered the bedroom, at the same time saying, "Hannah, I have a message for you from Juno. Hold off with the knife."

She replied, "It's not a knife, it's a dagger."

Bud could now see her eyes, and they looked clouded, muddled, like she was sleepwalking.

He continued, trying to stall until he could figure out some way to get the knife from Hannah.

"Juno says to tell you that you don't need to worry about ever seeing that ghost. Why don't you put the dagger down now, Hannah? It's kind of dangerous holding something that sharp close to your skin."

"Tell Juno I won't worry any more. And tell him the zombie will soon be dead. Everyone knew the zombie did it, yet I'm the only one with the courage to kill the zombie."

"That's very brave of you," Bud replied. "But Hannah, someone else killed Callie—it wasn't the zombie."

Hannah looked confused.

"Look, Hannah, do me a favor, please. Touch your throat."

Hannah did as Bud asked, touching her throat, yet still holding the dagger against it with the other hand.

"See, Hannah, that's *your* throat, not the zombie's. You don't want to harm yourself. Give me the dagger, Hannah. I'll kill the zombie."

Bud was beginning to falter. He'd had suicide prevention training as a law officer, but this was unlike any case he'd prepared for. Hannah truly seemed to be in some kind of trance. He wasn't sure what to do next.

"No!" Hannah yelled. "I'll kill the zombie. It's my duty, since I'm the one that saw the blood. Blood on the headboard! Blood on her forehead! And now blood on my foot! Enough is enough. I'll kill the zombie and throw her off the patio, like the zombie did Callie!"

Now Hannah's eyes looked wild, and Bud feared the worst. He was prepared to dive for the knife, but he knew she could do a lot of damage to herself before he could reach her.

"Hannah, I had a dream. Listen to me. You must do what my dream says, or Juno will be harmed."

Now Bud was grasping at straws, but he could see he at least had Hannah's interest.

"Juno's a good man," Hannah said, knife still at her throat.

"He needs your help, Hannah. Put the dagger down and come with me. We need to go help Juno."

Hannah hesitated. Bud knew it was his chance to go for the knife, yet he let it pass. He just wasn't ready and wanted better odds. He needed to be closer to Hannah to prevent her from hurting herself.

"No, you're tricking me," Hannah said. "I have to kill the zombie, then we'll go help Juno."

Hannah held the knife even closer to her throat, and Bud could see the muscles in her arm tense up. He knew she was mere seconds from killing herself, yet he was afraid to move.

Suddenly, in what seemed like a slow-motion dream, three blurs ran by the open patio door, three black and tan blurs with short legs, and the baying was so loud it made Bud's ears hurt. Hannah's eyes got big, and she suddenly looked confused.

Without even thinking, Bud dove for her, grabbing her arm and making her drop the knife. She tried to pick it up from the floor, but Bud was too quick and kicked it across the room, just as Juno came running in and had to jump to miss it.

Hannah now looked even more confused, and Bud could tell she was still in the trance.

Juno grabbed Hannah's arm and began leading her from the room, but Hannah pulled back and turned to Bud.

"I have something for your wife," she said, pulling a small jewelry case from her dress pocket and handing it to him. "I've been trying to get it to her for a long time."

Bud took it, then Juno led Hannah from the room via the patio door. Sprocket appeared below the deck with the hounds on leads, wearing a "don't ask" look on his face.

Bud put the case in his pocket and walked back down the hallway, returning to the party, which now seemed to be part of a different world.

He had no idea what had just transpired, but he knew that sooner or later, he would have to figure it all out and ask Sprocket and Juno, assuming he ever saw them again—or Hannah, for that matter.

## 46

Bud leaned back against the far wall of the castle's big ballroom, watching people dance to Howie and the Ramblin' Road Rangers. Most of the women had kicked off their heels, while the guys had taken off their formal jackets.

It sure seemed to Bud like a different crowd from the one he'd walked in the door with at the beginning of the party, and even the most stuffy and hoity-toity types had kicked back and loosened up.

Bud had seen Howie have this effect on people before at other gigs the band had played, even though this was their first paying one. It appeared to be a roaring success, and Bud was pleased with that, even though he was still trying to process what had just happened with Hannah.

Now Maureen was speaking into the microphone, and the crowd quieted. The disco light setup Howie had bought on eBay flashed its metallic lights, making everyone look surreal, reminding Bud of ghosts.

Maureen said, "As some of you may know, Howie is the Sheriff of Emery County, Utah, and when he's out on patrol on quiet days and nights is when he often has tunes come to him."

Bud grinned. Howie must write a lot of tunes, he figured, because there was seldom anything going on in Emery County.

Maureen continued, "When he found out we were going to be playing here in your beautiful valley, he wrote this song just for the occasion. It's dedicated to Doc and Millie Richardson, as well as to all you wonderful folks from Aspen. We hope you will take it in a spirit of fun and enjoy it."

She sat back down at the piano and started playing a honky-tonk tune, while Howie played a riff on his guitar and Barry strummed the bass. Soon, Howie began singing:

> I sat up all night,
> Hoping you'd do what's right,
> And call me, to come work for you.
> I can detail your car, wash your dogs, tend your bar,
> Even clean up your Viking stove flue.
>
> But you never called back,
> And I sure feel the lack,
> You could care less my rent's overdue.
> Yeah, you could care less my rent's overdue.
>
> I've got the working class down-valley blues,
> Wishing I could walk in your shoes.
> But I still have to say,
> You're a class act today,
> Cause you sent me a photo of you.
>
> I've got the worker bee down-valley blues,
> I just can't afford your kind of shoes,
> Yeah, the down valley working-class blues.

Bud was laughing even while wondering how the lyrics would go over with the glitterati from Aspen, but they loved it, whooping and yelling and asking for more and stomping and clapping in time.

Now a man came over and stood next to Bud, a fellow who looked just like some aging celebrity Bud was sure he'd seen somewhere, but not sure exactly where.

"Where do you live?" the man asked, smiling cordially.

"Down valley," Bud replied with a grin.

"Oh? Basalt? El Jebel? Carbondale?"

"No, I'm so far down valley it's not even on the Colorado map."

The man looked perplexed, shook his head, and walked off to dance with an attractive older red-headed woman who Bud swore was also an actress from somewhere or other.

Soon Wilma Jean was at Bud's side. "Hon, do you realize you just rubbed shoulders with the rich and famous?"

Bud examined his jacket. "Nope, wasn't aware of it."

She laughed. "You don't even know who that was, though they're famous. Aren't Howie and the band doing great? And we got a partial tour of the castle. It's incredible. I couldn't find you, though, where did you go?"

"Oh, nowhere much, just the usual, out keeping folks from killing themselves," he replied.

Wilma Jean smiled and nodded, then went across the room to talk to Millie and Doc. She was soon back at Bud's side.

"What did you say? Something about an attempted suicide?" she asked with concern.

Bud laughed. "That took awhile. No, all's well. I'll tell you about it later. I have something for you."

"What is it?"

"I'm not sure. It's from someone else. I'll dig it out later when we get home."

Bud knew if he told his wife it was from Hannah that she would fret over it until he showed it to her. He wasn't even sure what it was, but he didn't want to ruin Wilma Jean's fun.

He was still thinking about Hannah and what had just happened. It hadn't been the same Hannah as he saw all the time at the cafe, he knew that. She was different.

Now Bud remembered another part of his dream, where Howie had said he was so tired he felt like he was sleepwalking.

Bud wondered how he had overlooked that. If Hannah were a sleepwalker, it would explain a lot. He would be correct to think she would never see the ghost, for if she were sleepwalking, she *was* the ghost. And of course she wouldn't remember anything, like the morning she'd yelled weird cryptic stuff at him from her window above the cafe and then promptly denied it. She hadn't been lying, she truly was in a different state of consciousness.

From what Bud knew, somnambulism was a form of sleep disorder. You were awake physically, but not mentally, dissociated from the rational awake mind. He'd heard of people doing strange things, just like Hannah, and not being aware of their actions later.

In fact, he'd heard of cases where murder had been committed by people sleepwalking. He vaguely recalled some guy in Toronto who had murdered someone while sleepwalking and been acquitted.

Bud didn't know if Hannah had indeed murdered Callie, but if so, he figured she wasn't herself at the time, as the Hannah he knew seemed an unlikely candidate for killing people.

But one never knew. And Bud also suspected that Hannah had somehow dropped a piece of the castle's metal gutter on her foot, getting blood on it, then putting it in Dusty's car, for who knew what reason.

Bud was now startled out of his thoughts when the red-headed woman he'd seen earlier asked him to dance. He normally would have kindly refused, preferring to hang on the outskirts of social activities, but he'd been caught off guard.

Oh well, Bud thought as the woman led him out onto the dance floor. How many men could say they'd danced with a famous movie star, even though he didn't know who she was, especially to Howie and the Road Rangers' rendition of the 1964 hit by the Detergents, *Leader of the Laundromat?*

My folks were always putting her down,
Because her laundry always came out brown...

My dad said find a laundry that's new,
How can I tell my baby we're through?

All Bud recalled later was that he was laughing so hard he slipped and fell onto the dance floor, taking the star down with him, who in turn took down another couple who Bud was sure was also someone rich and famous, though he really didn't want to know. They were all helped up by Wilma Jean and Doc, everyone laughing.

It was an epic story, but one that was useless for retelling around the campfire because he knew no one would ever believe it.

The irony of it all was that Bud had never considered that song to be funny until that night. It must've been Howie's imitation of a country-western washing machine that had done it.

Anyway, Bud figured it had all turned out OK, unless he were to receive one of those "my people want to talk with your people" letters in the mail. If so, he figured he would just ignore it.

## 47

Bud woke with a groan, recalling the dance the night before, hoping it had been only a bad dream. He knew his wife would never let him live that one down, and, to top it off, both Doc and Millie had been there to witness his humiliation, as well as Howie and Maureen and Barry. He knew it would be all over Green River.

Fortunately, Howie and the band were on their way home, so Bud wouldn't have to endure any comments from that quarter. Maybe they would forget all about it by the time he saw them again.

He stretched a bit, then crawled out of bed, wondering where the dogs were. He could hear the sound of their little nails on the kitchen floor. Maybe he could get dressed and slip out to the cafe for coffee before Wilma Jean noticed and came in to remind him of the fool he'd made of himself the previous night.

Bud was quickly dressed and out the veranda side door when he noticed the cafe was closed. This was worrisome, though it didn't surprise him. He wondered where Juno had taken Hannah.

He resigned himself to his fate and went back into the cottage, then remembered the jewelry case. He would give it to Wilma Jean and sidetrack her before she could say anything. He took it from his jacket pocket and walked into the kitchen.

"Boy, you were something else last night," his wife reminded him before he could say anything. "You're lucky the paparazzi weren't invited, or you'd be all over the tabloids this morning."

She smiled that smile that Bud figured only knowing wives could smile as she handed him a cup of coffee, complete with a dollop of vanilla-bean ice cream.

Bud replied, "That's why the glitterati refuse to hang out with us down-valley types. They're smart."

"That's a heck of a way to meet people, hon," she added.

Bud shook his head, saying, "I'd rather forget it," as he handed Wilma Jean the case.

She took it tentatively, then slowly opened it. It held a locket on a long gold chain that was shaped like a heart, with a single ruby embedded in the center, a ruby of the richest red she'd ever seen. She slowly unlatched and opened the locket's lid.

Bud was now remembering something Sheriff Mason had told him some time ago:

*Let me know if you see a locket anywhere. Callie always wore a locket with a photo of her and her brother as children with their grandfather. It meant a lot to her, and it was missing after the murder. She wore it day and night, so someone had to have taken if off her.*

Bud watched, wondering what was inside. He could tell it was a very special piece of jewelry and guessed it held a photo of someone who had been very close to Callie. He still had no idea why Hannah had insisted it belonged to Wilma Jean.

As Wilma Jean studied it, she tried to speak, but her voice faltered, "Bud..."

"What's in it?" Bud asked.

"Bud," Wilma Jean's voice was barely audible. "Bud, I've never seen this one before. But why would Callie have..."

Bud was now by his wife's side, looking at the small photo in the locket.

"It's you and your Grandpa Wilson," he commented. "You must've been only about three then. He's even wearing that checkered beret he always wore, the one your grandma hated. And who's the little boy? He sure resembles Juno."

"Bud," Wilma Jean said, her voice now very soft. "Look closer. That's not me. My hair was blonde when I was little, but by the time I was that age, it had started turning darker. This little girl is still very much a towhead. That's not me, Bud."

"It has to be. It looks just like you."

"And look at the little turned-up nose, Bud. Mine's straight."

Wilma Jean was now carefully taking the photo from the locket. She turned it over.

"Little Callie, Sammy, and Gramps Wilson, Tumwater."

She looked at Bud in shock. "My grandparents lived in Tumwater, Washington before they moved out to Radium. Nobody ever talked about it, but I overheard Mom and Grammy talking about Aunt Jean, and how she'd given up her son and daughter for adoption."

Bud nodded, saying nothing, and Wilma Jean continued. "It was a taboo subject, and I seldom heard it mentioned again. Apparently her husband ran off with another woman, and Jean wasn't able to keep things together. She didn't tell the family until the kids were adopted, or they would've taken them. It was a sore spot for years for my grandparents. Callie was adopted by someone in the Seattle area, was all we knew."

Wilma Jean carefully closed the locket.

"It appears that Calico Callie was my first cousin, Bud. And possibly Juno, too, if that really is him. He must have changed his name. Who would've guessed?"

"My mom always said that cousins are sometimes more like each other than brothers and sisters," Bud said. "What a shame you didn't know before. But what happened to the little boy, her brother? Was he also adopted by the Seattle family?"

"No, he was adopted by someone who lived in Alaska. Both kids were totally lost to our family."

"It has to be Juno, then," Bud mused. "He said he was raised in Alaska. But the odds of them getting back together are astronomical. I wonder if they knew they were brother and sister?"

Thinking about things, Bud now felt even more confused than ever, if possible. Why did Hannah have the locket? Had she really killed Callie? This had to be what she'd been trying to give Wilma Jean all along, yet how did she know Wilma Jean and Callie were cousins? She had said the locket belonged to Wilma Jean, but it actually didn't, it was Callie's. Had Hannah, in her sleepwalking state, decided Wilma Jean must somehow be Callie?

The day had just started, but he was already tired. Yesterday had been a busy and eventful day, and all he wanted was to be back home in Green River, in their bungalow under the big cottonwood trees, watching his favorite TV show, Scooby Doo, and eating vanilla bean ice cream.

It seemed that something was wrong with a world where he was denied such a simple wish, Bud thought.

But they were leaving tomorrow, and Bud would have the day to recover. Doc and Millie had already returned to Palisade early that morning.

Bud left Wilma Jean looking at the locket and went into the bedroom. He pulled his boots off, put his coffee cup on the nightstand, then slipped back under the bed's big fluffy comforter.

All he intended to do all day was lounge around and read, even if the only reading material available was a book Wilma Jean had bought for a quarter at the Carbondale second-hand store.

It was titled, "My Life with Zombies: Living and Dying in Hollywood."

## 48

Bud had finally got some rest and was about ready to embark on what he considered the trip of a lifetime, even though it was one of his shorter trips of a lifetime.

He stood in the foyer of the Glenwood Springs Amtrak station, waiting for the big silver train to take him away, 85 miles down valley to Grand Junction. Wilma Jean would pick him up and take him to Doc and Millie's place in nearby Palisade, where they would spend the night.

He kind of wished he could just stay on the train until it got to Green River, but he knew he'd be back home soon enough.

Bud had been wanting to ride the train since they'd first come to Redstone, and now he was finally getting his wish, even though the darn thing was now running two hours late.

He wasn't sure what to do with himself while waiting. He'd already watched a big coal train idling, also waiting for the missing Amtrak train.

He'd then walked on the bridge across the river and watched the swimmers at the Glenwood Hot Springs Pool, but that got boring pretty fast, for if you've seen one bunch of kids splashing each other, you've seen them all.

He'd walked back down to the station when something occurred to him—maybe he could get in touch with Callie's attorney, Robert Daniels, Esquire, and see if he knew anything about what was going on. He knew Daniels' office was there in Glenwood.

Bud had tried to call Sheriff Mason earlier, as well as Deputy Schofield, but he'd been unable to get ahold of anyone. Now that he was finally leaving the area, he hated to not have closure on the Calico Callie case, assuming there was any to be had.

He found Daniels' number in the station's phone book and dialed. Daniels answered and seemed eager to talk to Bud, saying, "Juno called me and said that they arrested Gene Simpson. He admitted to killing Callie."

"That's good news," Bud replied. "I would really like to talk to Juno."

"I'll call him and ask him to call you, Bud. I don't have the authority to release his phone number to anyone."

"I understand," Bud said. "I just want to clear the air a bit and see what's happening, though I'm not sure anyone really knows the whole story. Did you know that Juno and Callie were brother and sister?"

"Yes," Daniels replied.

Bud was surprised. "Then Callie must have known that Juno was her brother."

"Yes, she knew. She recognized him from a picture she had of the two of them together when they were children. Callie's adopted parents told her that she was adopted and had a brother somewhere —they were very open about it all. When Callie bought the castle and met Juno, she knew it was him. She got a sample of his hair and had me send it in for a DNA test. There was no question after that."

"Why didn't she tell him?"

"She planned to, when the time was right, but she also didn't want to subject him to all the publicity that would come from being her brother."

"Do you think Juno knew?"

"No, I don't think he did. If he did know, he was very much to be

commended for not going after Callie's money and also for continuing to work for her. I need to ask him next time I talk to him."

Daniels continued, "Callie's will left her sister, Dusty, a nice trust.
She'll get $250,000 a year for life, which isn't too bad, in my opinion.
She also gets a nice house Callie bought as an investment here in
Glenwood Springs."

"That's great," Bud said. "But how about Juno?"

"The castle goes to Juno. It's valued at over 15 million dollars. She
also left him a hefty sum of money. And there's someone else in the
will," the attorney continued.

"Oh?"

"Callie left a beautiful house she owned in Tucson to Sheriff
Mason, as well as over two million dollars. She thought a lot of him.
And she left me $500,000. She was a very generous and kind person."

"Wow, sure sounds like it," Bud replied.

"But Bud," added the attorney. "That was only the beginning. She
left the majority of her fortune to various charities. Over 60 million."

"Sixty million dollars?" Bud was speechless.

"Yes. She was a very popular singer."

"That's amazing," Bud finally said. "But one last thing—did you
know my wife was Callie's first cousin? We're not interested in any of
Callie's money, that's not the point. I just thought you might find it an
interesting twist of fate, and I'd like for Juno to know he has a cousin
nearby. We'd like to stay in touch. Is there any way you could get that
message to him?"

"Of course, I'll be glad to tell him. I'd also be interested in
knowing more about it myself. Maybe Juno can fill me in after he
talks to you, if that's OK."

"Sure," Bud said. "But I'm really glad to hear about Gene, as I'm
leaving town soon, and I've been working on this case since I arrived
a month ago. It gives me some closure. Thanks for the information."

"You're very welcome," Daniels said.

Just then, Bud could hear the whistle of the Amtrak engine
coming down the track, and it was suddenly all he could think about,

just like a little kid. Callie and Juno and Hannah were quickly forgotten.

He was going to ride the big silver train.

## 49

The train had almost reached the little town of Rifle, a good 25 miles west of Glenwood Springs, when Bud's phone rang. This surprised him, as he somehow didn't think he'd have cell service on the train.

"Yell-ow," Bud answered.

The signal was a bit sketchy, but after they passed through a small canyon, it cleared up. Bud looked around to be sure he wasn't on an Amtrak Quiet Car, where cell phones aren't allowed. He didn't see anything that said he was, plus there was no one else in the car.

"Bud, Sheriff Mason here, and I have some news for you."

"You arrested Gene Simpson?" Bud asked.

"How did you know?"

"I just talked to Daniels. But in all honesty, I could have guessed it, as everything pointed to him—the dogs sniffing his car, the way he acted like he knew Dusty would inherit a fortune, the fact that he, as Callie's business manager, knew exactly how much that fortune was, the fishing lure found in her bedroom. Did the lab report come back on that yet?"

"No, but I know it will be conclusive. But we don't need it, Bud. The CBI searched his car and found a tie in the trunk covered with blood. He'd apparently been wearing it when he killed Callie. He thought he'd gotten rid of it, but it had fallen down into a crack and was hidden."

Bud replied, "Daniels said Gene confessed—he knew he had no alibi after you found the tie."

"Yes, his attorney is currently working out a plea bargain with the D.A. You can bet it will be a stiff sentence, given that Callie was such a high-profile figure. The D.A. doesn't want to lose his job. It will be quite some time before Gene Simpson sees life on the outside again."

"Did Dusty have anything to do with the murder?" Bud asked.

"Not that we know of. Gene said she didn't, and there's no reason to suspect she was there, no evidence. I'm overseeing the case again, by the way, now that he's confessed."

"Good. But what exactly happened?"

"You mean with the murder? Well, as near as I can piece things together, Simpson decided to kill Callie, thinking Dusty would inherit her money. He was pretty thick with Dusty and thought he would be set for life. So, he found a rock hammer, probably Juno's, and snuck into Callie's bedroom and hit her in the forehead while she was sleeping. Thankfully, I don't think she ever regained consciousness. All it took was one blow."

Mason's voice caught, and he stopped for a moment, then continued. "He told us he was planning on taking her body and dumping it in the river, but just then, someone came down the hallway, so he ran out the patio door. He couldn't tell us who it was, but apparently, whoever it was saw Callie and started chanting something really strange about blood."

Mason paused, then continued. "Gene could see them through the patio door, and he said it was a woman with a slight build. He watched as she took the locket from Callie's neck, then touched Callie's forehead, managing to get blood all over her hands. This would explain the handprint on the headboard. We fingerprinted it but the prints didn't match anyone we had on file. Strangely enough, they did match the ones on the piece of gutter Dusty found in her car. We figured they were Juno's."

"I think I know what happened, Sheriff," Bud said.

"What?" Mason was surprised.

"That woman was Hannah. She later dropped a piece of metal gutter on her foot, causing it to bleed. For some strange reason, she decided to put it in Dusty's car. Maybe the sight of the blood on it confused her and she thought it was the murder weapon."

"Why would she be in Callie's bedroom? Gene said she reminded him of a ghost. He said he later tried as he might to figure out who it was, but he couldn't. But you're saying it was Hannah?"

"It was," Bud replied.

Mason continued. "Well, the woman then left, and Gene went back in and was ready to deal with Callie's body, when he saw a man walking up the drive. It was Juno. We still haven't found Juno to confirm this. Gene said he didn't know what to do, so he threw Callie off the deck, thinking maybe someone would think she'd fallen, hitting her forehead. He then ran back behind the castle and took off his bloody jacket and tie and put them in his car trunk, later getting rid of the jacket in the river. He was in such a hurry that he forgot the tie. Juno saw Callie, and that's when he made the 911 call. It appears he was a bit drunk, making the call hard to decipher."

Before Bud could say anything, Mason added, "And yes, Bud, you were right. The voice analysis showed that Juno did say headboard, not forehead. I'm shocked that we all heard forehead, and even Dusty said she heard that when she talked to Juno on the phone. It was scratchy reception, but he did say headboard. So, he never actually even saw Callie's forehead to know she'd been wounded there, as he never approached the body."

Bud thought back to what Hannah had said when yelling at him from the window. She had known there was blood on both the headboard and the forehead, because she'd seen both.

Bud now said, "Juno then went into Callie's bedroom, trying to figure out what going on. He saw the hammer, then carefully picked it up with a plastic bag, thinking Hannah had killed Callie. He had to get rid of it fast, so he buried it out in the meadow, never thinking Gus Dearhammer might see him. And of course, Gene had no idea the fellow with the hounds would show up and sniff out his car."

"Makes sense," Mason said. "But once again, how does Hannah play into all this?

Bud answered, "Well, Hannah started having nightmares about blood on her hands. I believe she has what the shrinks call parasomnia, sleepwalking, and she went into a dissociative state every so often. I have no idea what set it off, but she would wander around at night. People would see her and think she was a ghost."

"Lady Bountiful's ghost," Mason said.

"Yes, and for some reason, she was wandering around the castle, which she'd done before, according to Callie's diary. After the trauma of seeing Callie's body, Hannah believed she'd killed her. But when she wasn't in this dissociative state, she didn't remember going to the castle and seeing Callie's body. When she was normal, she had no memories whatsoever of any of her night wanderings."

Bud continued, "Hannah somehow got the idea that Wilma Jean was Callie and that the locket she'd taken from Callie's body belonged to my wife. And through time, in order to make sense of it all and absolve herself of the guilt, as she'd seen blood on her own hands, she believed a zombie had killed Callie. Things got very confusing for her after that."

Bud could now see the big walls of Debeque Canyon in the distance through the window of the train car.

"I'm going to lose you soon, Sheriff," he said.

Mason replied. "Bud, how in the world did you figure all this out?"

Bud replied, "Well, it was actually pretty simple. I had a dream where Howie, my ex-deputy who's now the sheriff, said he was so tired he felt like he was sleepwalking. It finally dawned on me that Hannah had to be engaging in some form of sleepwalking."

Bud quickly told Mason about Hannah trying to kill herself and what had happened.

Mason replied, "How in hellsbells did Juno know what was going on, and also the guy with the dogs? It sounds like they showed up just in the nick of time."

Bud answered, "I talked to Sprocket later, and he said the dogs had simply gotten away from him again and headed for the castle. He's camped over on Gus's place. It was just coincidence, one of those things you find hard to believe. But Juno had been spying on the castle the whole time. I know because I would find his tracks every once in awhile. I think he was watching the whole thing, saw Hannah head for Callie's room, and cut around to the deck just in time."

Now Bud's phone crackled. He thought he'd lost Mason, then heard him say, "You still there?"

Bud replied, "Still here, but not for long. By the way, Callie and Wilma Jean are first cousins."

"What? I didn't quite hear you. They're frosted muffins?"

"First cousins!" Bud yelled as the train rounded a curve and entered the deep canyon.

"First cousins?" Mason repeated, his voice fading into the distance.

Bud leaned back. He knew it would take Sheriff Mason awhile to process what he'd just said. He looked out the window at the sight of the big canyon walls just above the train on one side and the river on the other.

Finally, he stood to go find the Cafe Car, hoping to get a cup of coffee, even though they weren't that far from Grand Junction.

As he stepped into the vestibule between the train cars, he turned back for a moment and noticed a sign on the door that read, "Car Closed."

No wonder he'd had the car to himself, Bud thought, grinning. He turned and went back into the car—the coffee would wait. He wasn't going to do anything that might compromise having a whole Amtrak car to himself. If the conductor saw him going back in, he might make him move.

Bud leaned back in the seat again and watched as the train now rolled through the little orchard town of Palisade. Bud would soon be at the Grand Junction station, where Wilma Jean waited for him, then they would come back to Doc and Millie's house near Palisade.

He would enjoy the last few minutes of the ride, pretending he was a hobo who had snuck into the closed car and was on his way to points unknown, free as a bird.

# 50

Bud and Wilma Jean sat in Doc and Millie's patio garden in Palisade, drinking homemade peach spritzer and munching on chips and homemade apricot jalapeño salsa.

Wilma Jean had picked Bud up from the train station the previous afternoon, and the couple had spent the night at Doc and Millie's. They would soon head to Radium, where Bud would begin his winter job working for his friend, Sheriff Hum Stocks.

"Man, you guys are going to spoil us," Bud said, tipping his anti-gravity chair back and nearly spilling his drink. "We can't grow peaches like this back home. This spritzer's going to give Old Man Green a run for his money."

"There's something about this area that creates a microcosm," Doc replied. "The humidity from the river and the big cliffs nearby create a place that fruit trees love. The rocks hold in the warmth, plus it's protected from the winds. Did you know Palisade used to be called Vineland?"

"Vineland? As in grape vines?" Wilma Jean asked.

"Yes, they used to grow wine grapes here, back before Prohibition," Doc replied. "They ripped them all out when alcohol became illegal. But now vineyards are becoming a big thing again, and a number of new wineries have been built. Colorado wines are getting to be quite popular."

"You should enter this peach spritzer in the fair," said Wilma Jean. "It's delicious. And your new raven marble sculpture really adds a lot to the garden, Millie."

"I love it," Millie replied. "Even though I've never seen a white raven."

Doc added, "We still go up on the Swell about once a month for a raven picnic. Millie has to go check on her birds and feed them. Those darn things remember her, after all this time."

Doc was referring back to when Millie owned the Ghost Rock Cafe up on the San Rafael Swell and fed the birds daily.

Millie laughed. "We drive over 130 miles one-way to feed the birds. Most people have feeders in their yard or just go down to their local park and feed the pigeons."

"It's a good excuse to get out," Doc added.

Just then, Bud's phone rang.

"Yell-ow," he answered.

"Bud? Bud Shumway? Do you have a minute? This is Juno Alaska."

Bud sat up straight, his chair popping back up.

"Of course I do, Juno. I always have time for family."

Millie and Doc and Wilma Jean all stopped talking.

"Family?" asked Juno. "Callie's attorney said you wanted to talk to me."

"Juno, can I put you on speaker phone? Wilma Jean and some friends are here, and we have a lot of questions for you, if you don't mind."

"Sure," Juno replied.

Bud turned on his cell phone's speaker, then asked, "Juno, did you know that Wilma Jean is your cousin?"

There was a pause, then Juno said, "Not until Sheriff Mason told me this morning when he called me. But I should've guessed, seeing how she looks just like Callie. Did you know they arrested Gene for Callie's murder?"

"Yes," Bud replied. "Mason told me. He also said you were off the hook. I wanted to call you yesterday, but didn't know your number."

"Well, you couldn't have called me anyway. I spent most of the day in Mason's office, getting interviewed—I turned myself in. But yes, they cleared me. I guess my timing was right, 'cause they had just arrested Gene."

Now Juno spoke softly, adding, "Thanks for taking my side on this, Mr. Shumway. Sheriff Mason said you maintained my innocence through the whole thing, and you were the reason they analyzed that 911 call a little better. Mason was pretty apologetic about that. But I never got the chance to thank you for leaving me food and a coat when I was up in the high country. It made a difference, you know."

"You're welcome, Juno. I hope you come visit us once in awhile, especially now that we know you're family."

There was a somewhat awkward silence, then Bud said, "Juno, did you know Callie was your sister?"

Juno replied quietly, "Yes."

"Did you know that Callie knew?"

"No, not that I was aware of, but I guess she did, since she left me part of her estate."

"You knew Callie was your sister, and she had tons of money and was very generous, yet you chose not to reveal yourself as her brother but rather to work for her as a lowly groundskeeper?"

"Nothing lowly about taking care of the castle grounds so others could appreciate it," Juno replied.

Wilma Jean, Millie, and Doc all sat quietly, listening.

Bud continued, "Don't you consider it an interesting twist that your sister bought the very estate you'd worked on for years? And yet she had no idea her brother worked there?"

"Fate's like that, Mr. Shumway. Sometimes the odds are against things, yet they still happen."

"Were you ever going to tell Callie you were her brother?"

Juno replied, "I had no plans to. I was happy enough being there for her. No need to upset the balance. Besides, I didn't want her to know her brother was such a loser."

"So you told nobody?"

"My adopted family knew I had a sister, but that was all. No idea who or where."

"How did you find out Callie was your sister?"

"She had a locket she wore all the time. But one time, she lost it out in the garden and asked me to keep an eye out for it. When I found it, I knew it was none of my business, but I had to see what was inside. She had a photo of us when we were kids with our grandpa. But I knew the tabloids would have a big party if they knew I was Calico Callie's brother. The twist of fate and all that. I felt better just keeping it to myself. I wish I knew what happened to that locket."

"Hannah took it when she found Callie's body, Juno. Wilma Jean has it. That's how we figured out Callie was related to Wilma Jean. You guys have the same Grandpa Wilson. We'll tell you the family history when you come visit. We're going to send it back to you, once we get your address."

"She has it? That's good news! But I talked to Callie's attorney, and he told me about how me and Wilma Jean were related. We talked about it for a long time, what Callie would want to do if she were still alive and knew. You know, Wilma Jean can keep the locket, it itself isn't something I want, but I wouldn't mind having a copy of that picture."

"We'll copy it and send you the original," Bud replied, then added, "Did you ever expect to get any of Callie's money?"

"No, I was happy with what I had. A good job, a nice place to live, and to be close to my sister—and to not have the paparazzi chasing after me like they did her."

"And now you own the castle. What are you going to do now?"

"I dunno. Maybe get a new car—and some decent shoes," Juno laughed. "I'm still wearing these stupid Goodyear sandals."

Juno continued, "I'll go back to living in my little apartment and taking care of the castle. It's a nice place. Sprocket's going to stay here and help me with it. Hannah's moving in, too."

Juno sighed, "But I've decided to sell the castle next spring and move back to Juneau. I miss the ocean. And I don't like the castle so much now that Callie was killed here. So I'll just move back to the ocean. But Hannah's going with me when I go, and we're going only if we can find her a good doctor. Do you think she'll be OK?"

"I don't know, Juno. I hope the doctors can help her. She's fine part of the time. If they can help her be fine all the time, she could lead a normal life."

"I'm going to keep helping her, I can tell you that," Juno said. "You know, Bud, when I saw Hannah standing there with that knife at her own throat, I felt a sense of deep despair like I've never felt. It made me realize what was really important in life, and it sure wasn't drinking. I didn't know what to do to stop Hannah, but I knew you were a trained lawman and maybe had dealt with situations like that, so I just hoped against hope you could handle it. Then Sprocket's dogs came running across the castle grounds like the hounds from hell, and I could see it was your chance. You did the exact right thing, and me and Hannah will always thank you."

Bud replied, "You know, Juno, Sprocket said he was going to solve Callie's murder, and in a way, he did. We would've never looked in Gene's car if his hounds hadn't sniffed it out."

Juno replied, "Yeah, that's true. I'll tell him you said that. But seeing Hannah like that made me realize she needed help. I was going to take her back to the cafe that night, but I just kept going on down the highway until I got to Valley View Hospital there in Glenwood, and I talked her into admitting herself into their psych ward. She didn't even know why she was in my car, had no memory of anything. When I convinced her I wasn't making it all up, she went on into the hospital. She has a really good doctor, Bud, and when she gets out, I'm going to keep a close eye on her. Dusty wants to buy the Ice House Cafe and turn it into a B&B. She's already moved into her house in Glenwood."

Now Juno laughed. "Hannah sure got a bit of a start when I finally convinced her she was Lady Bountiful's ghost. We were able to laugh about that one. But I heard you tell her I sent her a message that she didn't need to worry about seeing the ghost. I don't remember telling you that, Bud."

Bud replied, "You didn't, Juno. I dreamed you did, but I didn't tell Hannah it was a dream."

"Oh," Juno replied. "That makes sense, I guess. By the way, Dusty apologized to me, just so you know. She said she was mean to kick me out. I have to agree, but I would be mean to hold it against her."

Bud asked, "What did Dusty think when she found out about Gene?"

"Oh, she wasn't surprised. She said she knew he was a lowlife, but just didn't realize how low. He made all that stuff up about having an incurable illness just to get her to marry him. He's where he belongs."

"Agreed," replied Bud.

"Anyway, Bud, I know Callie would've left cousin Wilma Jean something in her will, had she only known. Me and Mr. Daniels think it's only the right thing for us to honor my sister's generosity by giving you guys some of her estate. He shuffled some money around, and said Callie would want that. One of the charities Callie had left money to went under, so we had some extra."

Juno paused, then continued. "Dusty told me she'd tried to hire you as a detective, and that you told her Wilma Jean was keen on buying an Airstream trailer and fixing it up as a spare bedroom. So, I called the Airstream company and set it up so you guys will have the biggest and finest airstream they make delivered to your place over there in Green River. All you have to do is call them with the date you want it delivered. It's already paid for, but if it's not what you want, you can change it."

Wilma Jean gasped, then said, "Those cost a fortune, Juno. You didn't have to do that."

"Hello, cousin," Juno said, laughing. "See, I have a vested interest, 'cause I want to come visit and have a nice place to stay. But it's not from my part of the estate, so I really didn't do anything, it was Attorney Daniels, he made it all work. And we think your friend who played the piano, what was her name, Maureen? She looks like Callie's stage costumes would fit her perfectly, so we'd like her to have them, if you think that's the thing to do. And I got Callie's diary back from Mason. You're welcome to read it, but it's going to stay in the family. Oh, I almost forgot, there's a check coming your way, too."

"Thank you so much, Juno. But have you thought about setting up a Calico Callie museum?" Wilma Jean asked.

Juno replied, "I thought about it, but I don't think Callie would've wanted that. She never was into any kind of self-aggrandizement. That's partly why we all loved her. Let her music be her legacy. But I gotta go. You guys are welcome to come visit at the castle anytime, you know that. Bring your friends. We'll drink spritzers and do some more dirt compression tests by throwing patio chairs off the deck." He laughed.

"That would be great," Wilma Jean said. "Whatever that is."

"Oh, I almost forgot one thing," Juno added. "You want that old convertible Callie had in the garage there? The red one with the white leather seats?"

Wilma Jean replied, "Oh my gosh! Of course, Juno, but I don't want it if you do."

"I'd be embarrassed to be seen in it, cousin. It's just not my style. I'm going to buy a used Toyota Yaris down in Glenwood. A man only needs so much stuff, after all."

"You can deliver it once we get the Airstream, come visit, then ride the train back," Bud offered. "It's a really fun train ride."

"Or we can take you home," said Wilma Jean. "Or even come get it. Not everyone loves trains like you do, hon," she added.

"Well, we'll work it out," Juno said. "You have my number now in your caller ID, so call me in a week or so. I gotta go see how Hannah's doing. Thanks again for everything."

With that, Juno hung up.

Bud and Wilma Jean looked like they were in shock, and Doc and Millie offered them another round of peach spritzer.

After they all talked awhile and tried to soak it all in, Bud finally said, "We need to get going. We have lots to do, and lots to think about. But now you guys will have a place to stay when you want to come feed the birds. No need to drive over and back in one day."

Wilma Jean added, "We're going to have a re-election party for

Howie in November, so plan on coming over then. By the way, Jill St. John and Robert Wagner were very nice last night. In fact, after we talked a bit, they said they're going to stop in next time they're in Green River."

She laughed and added, "That's one visit I don't think we need to worry about. They can stay in the Airstream if they do show up, but for some reason, I don't think they're in Green River very often."

Bud groaned. The thought of celebrities in his house was too much. He began fiddling with the beads around his neck, and Wilma Jean got up and walked over to him.

"Bud Shumway, I didn't know you wore a necklace! Since when?"

"My cousin sent it to me. It was my great-aunt Minnie Mae's."

"Looks like you have something new to fiddle with," she laughed, examining the necklace closely. "But Bud, those are Anglican prayer beads! I can't believe it. You're fiddling with your great-aunt's Anglican rosary. I guess nothing's sacred to your need to fiddle, is it?"

"I fiddle 'cause I have no choice. My brain won't work otherwise," Bud replied sheepishly. "It says so on the Internet."

Wilma Jean smiled. "You trust your brain to stuff you read on the Internet?"

She hugged Bud, then said, "I still can't believe all this is happening. I'm glad we decided to go spend some time in the Ruby of the Rockies."

"Me, too—I guess so, anyway," Bud replied. "Even though it wasn't much of a vacation."

They said their goodbyes, then walked out the door and on to better things.

———

# ABOUT THE AUTHOR

Chinle Miller writes from southeastern Utah and western Colorado, where she spends most of her time wandering with her dogs. She has an A.S. in Geology, a B.A. in Anthropology and an M.A. in Linguistics.

If you enjoyed this book, you'll also enjoy the other books in the Bud Shumway mystery series:

*The Ghost Rock Cafe*
*The Slickrock Cafe*
*The Paradox Cafe*
*The No Delay Cafe*
*The Silver Spur Cafe*
*The Ice House Cafe* (This is the sixth book in the series.)
*The Rattlesnake Cafe*
*The Beartooth Cafe*
*The Melon Rind Cafe*
*The Cessna Cafe*
*The Klondike Cafe*
*The Yellow Cat Cafe*
*The Swiftcurrent Cafe*
*The Sunnyside Cafe*
*The Temple Mountain Cafe*

And don't miss *Desert Rats: Adventures in the American Outback, Uranium Daughter, Wandering off the Map,* and *The Impossibility of Loneliness,* also by Chinle Miller.

And if you enjoy Bigfoot stories, you'll love *Rusty Wilson's Bigfoot Campfire Stories* and his many other Bigfoot books, as well as his popular *Chasing After Bigfoot: My Search for North America's Most Elusive Creature.*

Other offerings from Yellow Cat Publishing include an RV series by RV expert Sunny Skye, which includes *Living the Simple RV Life, The Truth about the RV Life,* and *RVing with Pets*, as well as *Tales of a Campground Host.* And don't forget to check out the books by Sunny's friend, Bob Davidson: *On the Road with Joe* and *Any Road, USA.* And finally, you'll love Roger Dean Miller's comedy thriller, *Bombing Hoffman.*

TY 9:30 2/27
W 11   3/1

Made in the USA
Coppell, TX
11 August 2022

81311496R00134